FIREKEEPER

FIREKEEPER

a novel

KATŁÌĄ

Roseway Publishing
an imprint of Fernwood Publishing
Halifax & Winnipeg

Development editing: Fazeela Jiwa
Copyediting: Rhonda Kronyk
Cover design: Ann Doyon
Text design: Lauren Jeanneau
Printed and bound in the UK

Published by Roseway Publishing
an imprint of Fernwood Publishing
Halifax and Winnipeg
2970 Oxford Street, Halifax, Nova Scotia, B3L 2W4
www.fernwoodpublishing.ca/roseway

Fernwood Publishing Company Limited gratefully acknowledges the
financial support of the Government of Canada through the Canada Book
Fund and the Canada Council for the Arts. We acknowledge the Province
of Manitoba for support through the Manitoba Publishers Marketing
Assistance Program and the Book Publishing Tax Credit. We acknowledge
the Nova Scotia Department of Communities, Culture and Heritage for
support through the Publishers Assistance Fund.

Library and Archives Canada Cataloguing in Publication
Title: Firekeeper : a novel / Katłįą.
Names: Lafferty, Catherine, 1982- author.
Identifiers: Canadiana (print) 20240309030 | Canadiana (ebook) 20240309065
| ISBN 9781773636573
(softcover) | ISBN 9781773636597 (EPUB) | ISBN 9781773636580 (PDF)
Subjects: LCGFT: Novels.
Classification: LCC PS8623.A35777 F57 2024 | DDC C813/.6—dc23

To all Indigenous women, girls and Two-Spirit people.

We are sacred because we exist.

— AUDREY SIEGL

in *Reclaiming Power and Place: The Final Report of the National Inquiry into Missing and Murdered Indigenous Women and Girls*

I write as a refusal to be silenced.

I write to resist shame.

I write as an answer to questions I'm tired of explaining.

I write to put down my side of the story.

I write because my manner of speaking is so slow.

I write in response to the narrative that knocks incessantly.

I write to put things down so I can move on.

— MICHELLE POIRIER BROWN
  in *You Might Be Sorry You Read This*

AUTHOR'S NOTE

This book was written during the pandemic while we were collectively on lockdown. As a result, there is a solemn melancholy throughout the story that meets moments of light. The main character, who is intermittently a version of myself from a life I no longer recognize and an amalgamation of many other people, suffers from agoraphobia. I wrote the harsh truths of a complicated character that cannot be defined or judged because, in one way or another, we are all Nyla. We all have an inner child that needs love.

For those who are sensitive to disturbing details of sexual exploitation and abuse, I want to caution you that this book has difficult moments of truth. While in the crux of writing this book, I found it very hard to separate myself from Nyla. Having to put my energy into the inner workings of her reality was not easy, but sometimes we have to go into the darkness to find the light. I needed to write about the experiences I have had and about the people I have encountered in my own journey in a way where I had control over the situation and could disassociate from those experiences in a healthy way. Not all experiences are my own. This is a work of fiction; however, some events and characters within are inspired by those I have crossed paths with throughout my life and I have gone to great lengths to protect their identity — even those who have hurt me. The characters in this book are not a depiction of any one person.

This book is a love story but not in the way you would imagine. It is a reflection of self, a search for inner wisdom, a connection to community; it is a journey back to ourselves through understanding that the very elements that can destroy us can also heal us, from fire to water to the very essence of what it means to truly love ourselves and others. This book is about letting go of what does not serve us. It was written for those who seek comfort in knowing we are much more than who or what the world tells us we are.

~

ONE

I used to live on the first floor of an old apartment building named after one of the first northern explorers who froze to death out on the ice, trying to make it to the top of the world. If only he knew how to make a fire to survive. It wasn't the cold that killed him and his men though. It was the scurvy. One of the only memories I have of my grandfather was when he told me the crew became zombies after the boat sank. He said they looked like the walking dead, and no one would open their doors to them for fear they might catch a disease.

It was just me and my mother, stuffed into a tiny one-bedroom apartment back then.

It feels like so long ago now. Like another life.

My bedroom was in the storage room. I had no window, just a loud, folding, sliding plastic door off the hallway. It looked more like one of those instruments ... what are they called? An accordion. Yes. A giant accordion.

My mom and I had just moved from a smaller community further north, a town close to where the explorer's boat sunk. My grandfather said that the people in the community knew exactly where the boat was all along, but the researchers that came looking for it every summer never listened to the locals and made up their own search instead.

When the boat was eventually found, it was because the researchers finally listened to the people in the community who led the researchers straight to it. Somehow, they still found a way to publish their own names in the papers, taking all the credit for finding it.

They left out the names of the locals, great hunters like my grandfather, who pointed it out to them. Their names were too hard to pronounce, I guess.

Now that I'm older, I've learned that's usually how it works in the North. People from out of town come up, name and claim things for themselves and call it discovery even though they are uncovering things that are not theirs to find or keep. Things that have already been "discovered."

My mom and I moved to Coppertown, the capital of the North, after my dad put her in the hospital. She was medivaced to Coppertown because her arm was broken so badly that the bottom half of it disconnected from her elbow and hung low towards her knee. She told me he had been holding me hostage the night it happened, after he kicked my mom out of the house. With no shoes on in the dead of winter, she had to run to the neighbour's house for help. I don't remember. I was only a toddler at the time. Apparently the only two police officers in our small community stood outside our rundown house in minus-fifty for hours, trying to get him to come out with his hands up. The officers had to take turns warming up in their idling police car.

I don't know why he did it, but my mom told me that when they finally got him to surrender, they found me watching cartoons and drinking my baby bottle full of pop, unaware of what was happening all around me. I'm just thankful my teeth didn't completely rot and fall out from the endless refills of sugary drinks.

My mom got pins in her elbow and had her arm in a cast. When the cast finally came off, her arm was permanently stuck in a bent position because she refused to do her physiotherapy.

Our small town didn't have a women's shelter at that time, even though it was much needed and still is. Domestic violence runs rampant in isolated places. When in Coppertown we were put up in a shelter and the workers helped my mom find a job and an apartment where we lived until I eventually left home if you want to call it that.

After we moved into the apartment when we left the shelter, my mom was never home long enough to spend time with me. I had the entire apartment to myself most of the time. Sick of staring at the wall in my small bedroom, it didn't take me long to find the crawl space underneath my bed.

A place to leave the world behind if only for a little while.

I often hid in there. Away from my mother. She was an angry drunk and even angrier sober.

I began to wonder if my father was as bad as she made him out to be. Maybe he had been trying to protect me from her the night he broke her arm. Maybe she had slipped and fallen on the ice. Had the police ever thought of that? I didn't want to believe he would hurt anyone. I wanted to have at least one parent to look up to.

My mother told me my dad killed himself. "Blew himself to smithereens," were her exact words. But it was an accident; I know it. I overheard her telling my auntie on the phone that he was trying to make homemade shatter, the equivalent of turning marijuana into glass through an extraction process, in the bathroom of his mistress's small housing unit. He was using a propane torch, and it exploded in his face. The newspaper said the entire structure of the house was ruined — the roof blown ten feet high into the air, the doors blasted off the hinges.

My mom drank the hard stuff. She sometimes drank for days. Random people came and went; some never left and just passed out where they sat in the living room. All I wanted was for everyone to leave, so one night I snuck into the kitchen and poured out what was left of the bottles and cans covering the kitchen counter. She'd still swig the leftovers even if there was a cigarette butt inside. She caught me in the act as the last of her precious booze drained into the sink.

"Nyla!" she screamed, and threw me into my room, where she tried smothering me with my own pillow. She was a hefty woman, so when she sat on my arms I couldn't fight back. One of her friends happened to walk past my bedroom on her way to the bathroom and

3

saw my feet kicking behind the half-open, smoke-stained plastic door. She pulled my mom off me and out of my room while my mom cried and screamed, pointing her finger at me.

"I wish you were never born!" she hollered over and over in a pitiful rage until she was out of breath.

She had tried so hard to end my life that night. The life she created.

When I discovered the crawl space, it became my escape. I would enter a different world down there underneath the four-storied apartment building held up by large cement cylinders. I had to duck my head and crouch under the pipes crossing in all directions, like a highway. I crawled over sand and rock, feeling my way in the dark with only the small glow of my storage bedroom lighting up the shadows.

I never went far past the entrance of my crawl space. I was too afraid to venture into complete darkness but learned that each unit on the ground floor had its own entrance into the crawl space. What might happen if I went into the wrong apartment? Maybe I would find a new mother. One that would hug me and never let me go.

Despite my desire to get away from my mother, I would always return home through the hole in the floor and shut the cover before she found out I'd been down there. My secret could not be exposed. It was the only escape I had.

It was the one thing I could not hand over to her. It was all I had that made me feel like I had some control of my own life.

There was another girl my age in the apartment building. I often saw her playing outside at the bottom of the hill, building a makeshift fort by herself. She worked on her fort every day after school with a hammer and rusty old nails, but she never got very far. When winter came, as it inevitably did, she abandoned her fort and went sledding.

The apartment building sat on the side of a hill. Vehicles had to drive up the big, steep, winding hill to get to the top, which made for the best snow hill. For the longest time I didn't know how much fun I could be having because I didn't go outside. It's not that I wasn't allowed; my mom probably wanted nothing more than for me to be out of her sight when she was home. It was more that I was afraid of going outside — of going out into the open. It's a fear I have struggled with on and off since I can remember. There's a name for it, I have since learned — agoraphobia. There's a name for everything nowadays. Agoraphobia left me conflicted, trapped between not wanting to leave my house but so desperately wanting to leave it at the same time.

Our apartment unit was situated in the middle of the hill, and I watched the girl through the ground-level living room window as she slid down on a piece of cardboard. I admired that she knew how to make her own fun.

Then one day, I heard her crying. I didn't see it happen, but when I saw her squirming and rocking back and forth on the ground, unable to get up, it was clear she'd slipped and fell on a patch of ice and hurt herself.

I had to help her somehow.

I tried to open the window, but it was frozen shut. The corners were covered in thick ice and pooled water from built-up condensation that spilled over the edge of the windowsill and down the paint-chipped white walls. When I looked out the window again it quickly fogged up from my breath. As much as I dreaded the thought of it, I had to help her, I had to go outside.

I tried to remember the last time I left the apartment as I searched for my boots in the back of the closet. I know I spent a few days in kindergarten, but then my mom stopped taking me when they started asking questions about why I was always late. When we first moved to Coppertown, she enrolled me in school only because she had to. At first, the school's automated machine called nearly every morning to remind her I was absent. But then the calls just stopped after a while. I guess they gave up.

I left my apartment with my boots on the wrong feet and no socks on. My light sweater wasn't enough to keep me warm, but I didn't plan on being outside for long. Thinking fast, I ripped a piece of cardboard from one of the unpacked boxes in the living room where my mother's belongings had been sitting for years collecting dust. As I left the building, I folded it and lodged it between the lobby door and the doorframe so that it wouldn't automatically lock.

"Are you okay?" I asked, already shivering as I met her on the hill.

"I can't get up." She squirmed. By then she had managed to flip herself over and was trying to crawl up the impossibly slippery hill on her elbows without touching the cold hard ground with her bare hands because her mitts had slid out of reach, halfway down the slope.

"Here," I said, picking up her mitts. I helped her put them back on while I rubbed my own hands together and breathed into them to keep my circulation going. "Grab my hand."

I helped her get to her feet. She limped and sobbed in pain as we hurried back up the hill to the lobby. But when we got to the steel door, the cardboard had fallen out. Someone had come and gone.

"We're locked out," I cried as the cold slapped me in the face. I suddenly felt the urge to pee.

"I have a key," she said, fumbling in her pocket.

Once inside, I asked, "Are you gonna be okay?"

"Yeah. Thanks," she said, embarrassed. "I'm Em. Well, my real name's Emerald. My dad says I'm his jewel." She rolled her eyes.

"Okay, well, bye." I didn't know to introduce myself and turned and ran down the hallway back to my apartment before I peed my pants.

I was secretly glad Em tripped and fell that day or else we might never have become friends. I wanted to hang out with her much more than I wanted to stay indoors, and I faced my fears every time she waved at me through the window to come outside. After a while, it got easier and easier, to the point where I nearly forgot I was afraid of being outside at all — as long as I was with Em. We never did go very far from the apartment. We would sit on the rocks under her window facing the sunset and splash our feet in the small pools of water after a good rain. We'd get bored and rip large weeds from their roots and throw them down the hill. In the sparse veil of the few trees that were left after bulldozing the land for development, we would find and step on hollowed out mushrooms that would shoot out a green powder.

"What's your name anyway?" she finally asked, after we had hung out a handful of times.

"Nyla. It's short for … something." I felt slightly embarrassed that I couldn't pronounce my full name. Since as long I could remember, my mom just called me Nyla. She told me my grandfather wanted to name me a name that in his language meant fire, which she thought suited me just fine because according to her, when I was a baby I screamed and screamed until I was red in the face. In my culture they say we choose our parents before we are born, but I couldn't fathom having chosen my mother. She jumbled up the letters of my original name to come up with Nyla for short. Just like the explorers didn't care to know our names, I didn't think my name really mattered much to my mother either back then.

Em grew up with her dad, who said her mom went crazy after she got what people now refer to as postpartum depression. In those days there wasn't a name for it. Em said she wasn't sad about it because her dad made up for her mom not being around. He spoiled his precious jewel by buying her whatever she wanted. Every other week, Em got to order clothes out of the Sears catalogue. She always looked so trendy.

"Sometimes," Em told me one day, "my mom will stand under my bedroom window and throw rocks, calling for me. But my dad just closes the curtains and pretends he can't hear her." As she spoke, she threw tiny pebbles at the ground. I could hear her hurt, but she masked it with a smile and changed the subject quickly. "Let's get started on our fort."

It was finally summer, and we could stay out longer. I picked up the hammer and nails, but then from out of nowhere I saw my mom coming up the hill. She was on her way home from a heavy night of drinking — doing, what she later joked with her sister on the phone, "the walk of shame."

"Nyla, your tits are going to sag when you're older if you play with hammers," she yelled between puffs of a cigarette. I put the hammer down until she went inside, then started banging even louder, hoping it would add to the wicked headache I knew she was going to complain about later. Maybe if I finished the fort, I could one day live in it just to get away from her.

It made me sad to know that Em had a mom that actually wanted to be in her life but was kept out. Then there was mine, who didn't want anything to do with me. If I had to choose between who was worse off, me or Em, I guess I'd say me because at least Em knew her mom loved her.

I only ever really talked to Em's dad a handful of times. The only times I remember him being nice to me were on the occasions when I got hurt. Like when Em and I were playing on the rocks behind the apartment, pretending we were professional rock climbers. I tried to show her up by climbing a steep cliff, but when I got halfway up, I could no longer carry my own weight. I had nowhere to put my feet for support and my grip slipped. I fell to the ground right next to a sharp, pointy rock. If I'd fallen a few inches over, I probably would have been paralyzed. Em must have thought it hurt worse than it did because, as I was about to get up, she started screaming for her dad, whose living room window was just above where we were climbing. So I decided to act hurt.

He quickly came down around the side of the apartment building to see what happened and assess the damage.

"Can you walk?" he asked.

"I don't think so," I lied. I wanted to be taken care of, I guess. To my surprise, he picked me up and carried me all the way back to the couch in their apartment. He got Em to bring me an ice pack to put on my back.

"I'll call your mother," he said, walking towards the kitchen.

"She's not home," I lied again, getting up quickly. "I'm okay now," I said and ran out the door.

It was nice to know what it might have felt like to have a dad, if only for a time.

I remember Em gave me a professional portrait of the two of them as a Christmas present one year. She was tucked under his shoulder and her head leaned on his chest as she stood on a chair to meet his height. His body language said he would always protect her, and it made me jealous. I crumpled it up and threw it in the garbage.

～

My mom smoked a lot. She always left lighters lying around the apartment. The first time I got hold of one, I spent the entire night flicking the small wheel off and on in the dark of my bedroom. I just lay there, staring at the blue and red flame until my thumb was numb and I couldn't hold the wheel down anymore.

Growing braver, one day I managed to steal a few of my mom's cigarettes from the back of the freezer where she kept them, thinking the cold would keep the tobacco fresh. I didn't want to try smoking alone so I tried to get Em to smoke with me. When we met up in the elevator, I handed her a long skinny white menthol.

"No, it's all right," she said.

"Come on."

"No, I don't want to." She put the back of her hand up in front of her mouth to shield herself from me.

I hit the emergency stop button and cornered her. For a moment I held the burning end of the lit cigarette so close to her eye I could have nearly burned her blind.

"Whatever," I breathed, as I blew a cloud of smoke in her face like a movie star.

Em pressed the button for her floor in a panic, and when the elevator doors opened, she ran out, trying to hold back tears. I didn't care then, but later that evening I started to wonder why I did it. I was supposed to be her best friend. Best friends don't do that to each other, I knew that. Was I becoming like my mother?

No. I would never allow it.

That night, I burned myself to try and rid the guilt and regret of what I'd done. I let the steel end of the lighter heat up until it was red hot, then I pushed it hard against my cheek. The pain rang through every cell in my body, telling me to stop, but I fought off the voice and pressed down even harder until my skin brought the lighter back down to room temperature, leaving a blister in the shape of a horseshoe on my face. The scar eventually faded but it's still noticeable under certain light or in cold weather, like a case of bad frostbite.

To my surprise, Em forgave me a few days later. I thought she would never speak to me again, but she was the forgiving kind, which made me feel like I didn't deserve her. I knew Em secretly wondered if maybe my mother gave me the blister, but she never directly came out and asked me. Maybe my own mother wondered if she did it to me too, in one of her drunken rages.

We gave up on the fort as we got older. Eventually our daily meet-up spot moved to the steps of the empty stairwell on the far side of our apartment building. I listened intently to Em day after day as she went on about her mother while I tried to blow smoke rings. One day, as Em was talking about how her dad said her mom shook her when she was a baby, I'd had enough and interrupted her woes by jumping off the steps.

"This is for your mother," I said, and proceeded to start a small fire in the blue faded carpet at the bottom of the stairs.

"What are you doing?" Em ran over to the flames and stomped them out. "Are you crazy? What did you do that for?"

I just shrugged and laughed, "It's out. Relax."

After that, I made small fires everywhere I went. I even set off aerosol spray cans, the kind that make your house smell nice. We didn't have any at my house, but Em's dad always had one next to the toilet. I learned through trial and error that if you hold a lighter up to the nozzle while pressing down on it, the spray can would light up like a flamethrower. Em would have to open her bedroom window so the flames had somewhere to go. The first time I did it she freaked out, but after a while she got used to the crazy things I did when we were bored. She even tried it herself.

"See, I told you it's fun," I said, watching as she held the spray can as far away from her body as possible and turned her face away.

"If you can't beat 'em, join 'em!" she said with a shrug.

For Em, fire was something to be feared. For me, fire was a desire. I was completely drawn to it in the same way that people are drawn to an addiction. I would revel in the flames I created. Sometimes, I would run my hand over the heat quickly; other times, slowly, to see how it felt to feel such warmth. It was comforting.

It was a pain I could control.

Lying in my bed at night, I eventually figured out how to empty out the gritty charcoal inside the lighter by winding the grinder up backwards until there was enough residue built up to pour the contents out. I tipped the powder out onto the glass surface of the cheap patio table that was my nightstand, tapping the lighter to let the crackling powder pile up. I gathered the salt-and-pepper dust on my thumb and middle finger and snapped it over the lighter's flame, causing sparks that looked like tiny fireworks. It was the same stuff they used for those sparkly candles on Em's birthday cake that set the smoke alarm off in her apartment and made everything smell like rotten eggs.

When my mother wasn't home, Em would sometimes come over and bring her assortment of catalogue clothes in a fancy rolling suitcase. We would dress up and pose like models while listening to music with her stereo blaring the latest mixtape she made.

"Wanna see something cool?" I asked her as we lay around in my bedroom atop a pile of colourful clothes that covered the floor — clothes that neither of us would ever be brave enough to wear out in public. I wore a dark green, velvet body suit and she had on a sequined ball gown that was too big on her. She had ordered it with plans to one day graduate in.

"Sure," she said, naively opening herself up to my dark world without knowing it.

I trusted Em. I trusted her so much that I wanted to show her my secret. I wanted to share with her the one place I swore I would never let anyone else know about. When I opened the latch to the crawl space under my bed, Em was cautious. "What's down there?"

"Nothing, it's just cool down there," I said innocently. "It's not much of a jump. It looks hard but it's pretty easy if you don't overthink it."

The floor wasn't far from the ground, but the first time I lowered myself through it, I nearly bounced my face hard off the edge. It was a very small, square hole, so you had to jump at just the right angle and time your jump so that you didn't hit your chin on the opening or knock your shins on one of the long silver pipes inside.

Em got up the nerve to join me once I lowered myself in. She made it down in one piece with a little guidance and stared at me with a scared look in her eyes.

"How are we going to get back up?"

"Don't worry, I'll boost you up."

"Can you leave the door open for light?" she asked when I was about to slide the wooden frame over the hole. I had gotten used to being in complete darkness.

"Sure, but we're safe down here. No one can hurt us."

She looked at me, puzzled. "Who would hurt us?"

"Never mind," I said.

"Do you spend a lot of time down here?" she asked, taking a sudden interest in my life, wanting to talk about me instead of her for once.

"No," I lied.

After a pause, she finally came out and said, "She's mean to you, isn't she? Your mom?"

"No," I lied again. I don't know why I felt the need to lie to Em. Maybe it was to avoid having to admit it to myself, to protect myself from the truth.

"Why'd you bring me down here? I mean it's cool and all, I guess, but it's weird," she said. She tried to stand up but there wasn't enough room. "What are all these pipes for?" she asked, following one of them with her hand.

"I think they're just full of gas or maybe water. Let's find out." Without thinking of the consequences, I fished for the yellow lighter in my pocket. I looked over at Em who had inched her way back to the opening. She was standing up straight with her head peeking out, trying to figure out how to get out.

"I think I'm feeling claustered," she said.

The small flame from my lighter lit up the dark and Em turned and ducked to see where the light was coming from.

"What are you doing?" she asked when she saw me holding the flame up to the pipe.

I didn't answer. I was too preoccupied with wondering if that was all it would take to blow up the building, just one small flame.

"Nyla!" Em shouted to get my attention.

I took my thumb off the trigger.

Though it was just a fleeting thought, this marked the beginning of my distorted curiosities.

I quickly stuffed the warm lighter back into my pocket. "It's harmless. It's mostly just water running through these things anyway," I said, knocking on a hollow-sounding pipe.

Em stared at me in disbelief, suddenly sounding more like an adult than a kid, "Were you trying to kill us?"

"No," I said defensively. I tried to laugh it off.

"Just get me out of here," she demanded.

I didn't try to talk her out of it. I respected her wishes, even though I could have stayed down there longer. Together we could hide away. The crawl space was a place where life didn't seem to exist at all. Not even a spider. Just a long stretch of sand and rock from one corner of the building to the other.

I hoisted Em back up through the floorboards, letting her step into the palms of my hands as I fought to keep my fingers interlocked. Once she was out, I lifted myself up without help. By then, I had gone down there so much on my own that I could get up and out easily.

Em didn't speak to me for a while after that, and I stopped going down into the crawl space. Not because I wanted to stop, but because my mother caught me down there — I'm assuming Em told her dad about it, who must have told my mom.

I was deep down inside, exploring the hilly part of the crawl space, when I heard my mother's angry stomp coming closer and closer until the floorboard cover slid open. She got down on her hands and knees and stuck her head through the square hole. Looking like she was about to do a push-up, holding onto both edges of the hole, she yelled my name angrily.

"Nyla!"

I didn't answer. I crawled backwards as far back as I could go, trying to slide between the pipes until the space between them became too narrow.

I knew she wouldn't come in after me. At least I was safe in that sense. But she shut me in and waited, knowing I would eventually have to come out. Out of both stubbornness and fear, I sat there for hours until I couldn't take it anymore. I was hungry, thirsty and out of lighter fluid.

I didn't leave the apartment at all that summer. The fear of leaving my bedroom had found me again.

TWO

Em and I continued to be best friends, but after the crawl space incident her dad didn't want me hanging around with her anymore. She had to lie that she was going out with friends from school just so she could spend time with me. On the days she didn't have her after-school teen program and her dad was still at work, I would sneak over and hang out at her apartment.

When rollerblades were all the rage, her dad bought her a top-of-the-line pair. After school, I met her on the corner down the hill from our apartment building, which was hidden behind another smaller apartment, so she could show them off. I would run to keep up with her while she rollerbladed fast ahead of me. She was only good on flat surfaces. Unable to go uphill or down, she would lean on me or hold my hand for support whenever she reached a small incline. On a long stretch of good sidewalk, she acted like a pro, but I had to help her up whenever she hit a crack or groove. Her elbow and knee pads protected her from getting road rash.

"I heard the queen's in town," she said excitedly after learning how to spin on her blades.

"So?"

"The queen and her husband, the duke."

"Why is he called a duke? Why not a king?" I asked.

"I'm not sure. I guess maybe he doesn't want to be a king."

That didn't make sense to me. "Who wouldn't want to be a king?"

"My dad said they went around in helicopters and sprayed Coppertown to keep the bugs away just for them."

"Is that why I haven't seen one mosquito yet this summer? What if they come back with a vengeance?"

"Oh Nyla, why do you have to complain about everything? You'd be complaining about bug bites right now if it weren't for the queen. Let's go see her."

I honestly didn't care to see any members of the royal family, but Em was adamant on going to the hotel they were staying at — the only fancy hotel in town — and of course, I reluctantly followed. When we got there, shiny black town cars were lined up outside the hotel lobby and a narrow red carpet was rolled out on the dusty unpaved ground in front of the hotel's sliding doors.

Em would have been jumping up and down with excitement if she weren't so unsteady on her rollerblades. I'm pretty sure I yawned as the queen was helped out of her town car followed by a man I could only suspect was her husband. Without thinking I shouted, "Hey, Duke!"

He turned and looked at me in surprise, and the queen waved her strangely cupped, white-gloved hand at us robotically. Em was mortified and sped away down the small wheelchair ramp, flailing her arms like a bird to keep her balance. I ran to catch up to her.

"Why'd you do that?" she asked angrily.

"I wanted to be sure he was the duke and not a king!" I quipped innocently, not understanding what the big deal was. She sped home, giving me the silent treatment as I tried to keep up.

Em never stayed mad at me for very long though, and by the time we got back to the apartment she had forgotten why she was upset.

"I wish we could hang out more," she said before we parted ways next to the old broken-down fort held together with long, rusted nails. We'd given up on trying to fix it.

"It's never gonna happen. Your dad hates me."

"Hey, I have an idea. Why don't we sleep in the school? I can say I'm sleeping over at Kayley's house."

Kayley was her other best friend who always seemed to find her way into our conversations. She sounded smart and pretty, and Em said she wore her hair a different style every day.

"Where'd you get that idea?" I asked, thinking maybe she saw it on one of the shows her and Kayley were always talking about. Not having cable, I was left of the loop about their favourite characters.

"I just thought of it. It'll be fun!" she said.

"Yeah, sure. Why not?" I said, trying to match her enthusiasm.

I met Em after school at the end of the week as planned. I paced the hallway outside of her classroom trying to look like I was a student on a bathroom break.

I hadn't stepped inside of a school since elementary, but I didn't feel like I was missing anything. I could still read, just not very well. I knew the words that were necessary. Words like "stop" and "exit" in big bold letters, or names of stores and restaurants that I heard Em referring to and recognized in magazines. I tried to sound out words in my head whenever I would see familiar letters side by side. As for math, I counted with my fingers just fine on the rare occasion that I had enough change to buy something at the corner store. Ten fingers was all I needed to know about math.

Em asked me to meet her at the back door of the school near the portable, but standing around and waiting always made me have to pee, so I went inside to find a bathroom.

When Em saw me, she quickly walked out of her classroom and whispered, "What are you doing here? You're supposed to wait outside."

"Sorry, I had to go."

When she saw the teacher heading towards the door she said, "Go. Hide behind that door, quick. The teacher's going to ask me who you are."

I ran and tucked myself into the space between the wall and

door, which had just enough room for me to hide in before the bell rang and the students filled the hallways. The door had a window in the top half with tiny squares of mesh netting inside the glass that made me feel dizzy when I reached up to peek through it.

I waited until the commotion dwindled. I waited and waited until I thought that maybe Em forgot about me, until she came running up and slid to a stop in front of me, pushing into me she as far as she could. She barely had enough room to tuck her feet in before the janitor walked by.

Taking a break from his rounds, the janitor walked into the open area, straight past the door we were hiding behind. He whistled as he stood looking out the window into the schoolyard with his hands on his hips. He stood there for so long I worried I would sneeze. He was sure to see us huddling together behind the door when he turned around, but to our surprise he just walked on past us and a few minutes later we heard him turn his loud vacuum on.

Em waited a few more seconds before letting out a giggle. "That was close."

"I can't believe he didn't see us. He looked right at us," I said in shock.

We waited a few more minutes until she said, "Follow me."

She carefully walked over to her locker, peeking around corners and making sure the janitor was gone before making any sudden movements. Only after the lights started turning off, except the emergency exit signs that lit up the hallways in a red glow, followed by the sound of a set of keys jingling behind a heavy door slamming shut, did Em sigh with relief.

"Did you bring the stuff?"

"What I could find. Sandwiches, beef jerky, chocolate milk, sour keys," I said, rifling through the white plastic bag of goodies that she gave me money to buy.

She stowed the food away in the top shelf of her locker and closed it quietly. "Good. C'mon."

Neither of us were sure of what to do next. Now that our plan had worked, and we were actually in the school after hours, we weren't so sure if we wanted to be there anymore.

"What should we do now?" Em turned to me. "We've got the whole school to ourselves."

I shrugged. This was her idea, not mine.

"It's kind of spooky in here. Sort of like your crawl space."

"Yeah." I pretended to laugh.

"It's still really early." The daylight spilled in through the windows and lit up sections of the dark hallways leaving thick horizontal shadows across the floor.

We walked to the same window where the janitor stood, and for a while we watched some teenagers playing basketball on a run-down court in the middle of the schoolyard.

"Let's go to the library," Em said, bored with watching the boys miss the net over and over.

Neither of us was into sports. We weren't into reading either, but we went to the library anyway. I picked up the thickest book I could find and plopped down on a beanbag chair.

"How do people find this interesting, anyway?" It made me feel in control of my weaknesses to lie, but deep down I wished I knew how to read. Wished that someone would take the time to teach me. Em could read no problem but chose not to. She just fanned through comic books like she did her clothes catalogues.

The library was one big open space above a large set of floating stairs facing a mezzanine that looked sort of like an indoor courtyard. The high ceilings made me feel small. Like something larger than life was watching us.

"Let's go check out the gym." Again, we were on the move.

We pushed open the heavy, wooden double doors and tiptoed into the gym.

"They keep the fun stuff in here." Em led me to the unlocked storage room and we dug around in the large wooden bins, grabbing whatever we could. We tested out all the different sports equipment — skipping ropes, a parachute, square flat pieces of wood on wheels — until we got bored again.

"Where are we sleeping?"

"Up there." Em pointed to the stage at the front of the gym.

"On the stage?"

"Yeah. I'll show you."

I followed her up the narrow steps on the side of the stage. Behind the long red curtains was a ladder that led to a loft where the drama club's theatre props were stored. We climbed up and found a pile of large, blue, plastic mattresses.

"We'll sleep on these," Em said.

I flung myself down on the hard plastic, thinking it would be a soft landing. It wasn't. "Ouch."

I laughed as Em joined me, landing much more gracefully. She explained that she had the role of a woman jumping off a bridge to her death in an upcoming play for her afterschool program and had to practice the jump from the stage onto the mat.

"That sounds morbid," I said, copying the word from Em, who regularly called me morbid.

"It's about a girl who wants to end her life and her best friend says she will jump with her, but at the count of three the girl changes her mind but the best friend doesn't realize it until it's too late."

"Like I said, morbid."

It was still early, but for some reason we thought we could close our eyes and fall asleep under the bright neon lights and stillness of the stale, smelly gym. In no time, it proved impossible. So we climbed back down and shut the gym lights off one by one until it was so dark I couldn't see my hand in front of my face. I lit my trusty lighter to find our way back to the loft. Neither of us had thought of bringing a flashlight.

"It's so dark in here," Em said shakily.

"Kind of like the crawl space," we said at the same time.

"Worse." Em shuddered.

Another few minutes went by and not a sound could be heard except the plastic mat shifting underneath us every time we moved an inch.

"We don't have any blankets," Em said.

"What time is it anyway?" I asked, not that it really mattered.

"I don't know. Let's look outside."

We climbed back down into the gym and pushed hard on the silver bar that ran across the emergency exit doors, which opened out onto the kindergarten play area. The sun was still high in the sky.

"Wow, it's still really early."

"You still want to do this?"

"Do you?"

I shook my head and made a face of disapproval.

"Me neither."

We ran outside and watched the boys play basketball until dark. When Em opened her locker on Monday morning all she could smell was sour milk and mouldy sandwiches.

Breaking into the school wasn't the only dangerous game we played. That summer we learned how to play a game aptly called chokey. Em's dad had booked the same campsite every weekend of the summer and I would walk all the way there on the highway to hang out with her. It would take me nearly half the day to get there just to meet her at the playground on the beach at dusk while her dad sat alone by the fire roasting hotdogs. The beach was adjacent to the airport and every few hours a plane would fly loudly overhead, drowning out the noise of us kids playing across the dusty, gravel roads that led sporadically through rows of semi-secluded campsites. Between running barefoot, burying ourselves in the sand, and jumping off swings in mid-air, we met up with a group of kids who were playing chokey.

"How do you play it?" Em asked judgingly.

"You just choke each other until someone passes out," said one of them.

There really was no point to the game other than showing how brave you were or how much you trusted the other person to stop strangling you at the exact moment, right before it's too late. We watched as one boy got choked by his cousin until he closed his eyes and fell into the soft sand. When he slowly came to, he got up in a craze and chased us around. He had somehow transformed. He chased us demonically, and I feared what would happen if he caught one of us. But he never did because the trance only lasted a few minutes until he passed out again and woke up as himself.

Soon enough Em and I found ourselves part of the game with our newfound friends, both of us scared yet intrigued by what might happen. When it was my turn, the world turned dark and I fell to the ground. When I awoke, I felt no different, but I knew the kids would be expecting me to be possessed. With a sore neck, I had permission to be wild but I took it too far. To my surprise, I went for Em with an anger summoned from somewhere inside that I didn't know even existed. I grabbed the first weapon I could find, a long strip of wood from a construction zone on one side of the park that was blocked off with orange pylons and yellow caution tape. The two-by-four was heavy, but I dragged it across the sand making bizarre animal noises. The kids were all screaming and running, some of them laughing through fear.

"What are you going to do with that?" one of them taunted.

Em hid behind one of the pillars in a nearby gazebo and thought I didn't see her, but I waited for her to poke her head around to see where I was. That's when I swung. I hit Em square in the forehead with the flat end of the two-by-four and she fell to the ground instantly.

I wish now that Em's dad had been there to stop us from playing such a demented game.

In keeping with my performance, I collapsed back on the ground. I waited for one of the kids to come over to me to see if I was okay, but no one did. Pretending to snap back to reality, I sat up rubbing my head and asked, "What happened? Where am I?"

But everyone hovered around Em, who wasn't moving.

Did I kill her?

It felt like time had stopped but relief washed over me when I saw her move. The kids collectively gasped and stepped back when she got up, worried she might have turned into a monster. As if my touching her with another object would turn her into a zombie. She definitely looked like she was back from the dead. She had a large goose egg protruding on one side of her forehead. It was already a deep purple and full of red veins from swelling so quickly. I couldn't look at her without having to look away.

Everyone turned to me.

"Look what you did!" said one of the kids angrily.

"It's only supposed to be a game!" cried the one who made it up.

I couldn't even apologize. I wanted to throw up. I wanted to run away and so I did. I ran all the way home without stopping.

I'm sure that was the last time any of those kids played chokey. I don't know how Em explained what happened to her dad, but I know she didn't tell on me because he hadn't come banging on my door like I anxiously anticipated he would. I wanted to be punished. I didn't care if I got in trouble. All I cared about was that Em was still alive.

That was the last time I remember being a kid. Shortly after that, Em and I grew up. One day we were just children playing, and the next we were teenagers with breasts. Or, as I called them, boobs.

I hated my boobs. They made me feel uncomfortable. When I first noticed they were changing, sticking out an inch off my chest all pointy and weird-looking, I didn't even want to look at myself in the mirror. But I wasn't able to look away either. I didn't want my body to change without my permission. I didn't want to grow up into a woman. I didn't want boys to look at me. I didn't want to be attractive.

Luckily, I was a late bloomer and got my period well after Em did. I just wasn't ready to deal with the troubles that came along with having a period after hearing the horrors that Em was going through.

Unfortunately, puberty wasn't the worst thing that happened to me that year. A boy tried to come between Em and me. Noah was his name and he managed to weasel his way into Em's life before I could stop him. I didn't like him from the start. Him or his friends, but mostly just him. He showed up out of nowhere on the day Em persuaded me to go to the beach with her. It was the hottest day of the decade on record, and the mosquitoes had come back with a vengeance, as I had predicted.

Em and I were sitting chin-deep in the clear lake water at the end of the beach, as far as we could go without having to worry about leeches in the marshy part. We let the waves hit our shoulders, nearly knocking us over while we tried to keep our feet afloat. We both had the same bright-red toenail polish on, and I had a head full of a thousand small braids with beads on the ends.

"Sit still," Em had said while she braided each strand of my unruly hair the day before. I would have braided her hair too but was too impatient to learn how. It took hours, but Em said it would be a good way for me to keep my hair under control and out of my face. I know I got my wavy hair from my dad, even though I don't remember what his hair looked like. My mom had stick-straight black hair as harsh as her hardened face.

I had always seen Em as the pretty one, and now so did Noah. He came up to us in the water, took a handful of wet sand, and threw it in Em's direction, barely missing her on purpose.

When the war broke out between the boys and the girls that day in the water, Noah only targeted Em, and next thing you know she was on his shoulders laughing and squealing with fear and excitement as he threw her backwards into the air where she landed in the water over and over. It was hard to watch.

No one cared to throw a wet mud ball at me, and no one noticed when I walked back over to my beach blanket. The sand stuck to my wet feet and legs as I plunked down on my towel in a soggy heap, a perfect description of what I felt like inside.

I hated the beach. I hated cold water. The only reason I went to the beach that day was because Em wanted me to go with her to "check out boys." If I'd known how it was going to be, I would have stayed home and stared at the ceiling, chipping off the two-week-old red nail polish that Em had painted on me.

Noah was a typical show-off. I watched from afar as he did elaborate backflips and somersaults off the cliffs. I hadn't wanted to go all the way out to the cliffs, but when the group decided to go, I ended up tagging along, dragging my feet as we hiked a half mile to the other side of the lake. There was no way I'd leave Em alone with a bunch of boys even if she didn't notice me.

The stage was set that summer whether I liked it or not. Day after day, and into the night with the light of the midnight sun, the other kids all jumped off the cliffs. Even Em did cannonballs while I sat back with a growing jealousy that I couldn't help.

Closer towards the end of the summer, the boys gathered up their courage and bravado and dared one another to swim to the other side of the lake.

According to them, few people ever made it from the cliffs to the dock on the other side of the lake near the airport. I sat up a bit straighter, taking more of an interest in their boastful overconfidence. A part of me secretly wished Noah would get a cramp. By that point I loathed him. I didn't only despise Noah because he was a braggart that was taking my best friend away. I had a special hatred for him after I found out how he treated animals. I didn't ever care much for rodents but one evening at the beach, he casually told us what he did to his pet hamsters. He laughed about watching them drown in the bathtub. I was surprised that Em didn't see that sinister side of him.

Or maybe she just ignored it, like she probably did with me, because she was always making plans with him and his friends.

I watched as Noah's friends made it as far as the middle of the lake and couldn't go any further because they were too tired, but Noah kept going. His friends treaded water in a panic until a canoe happened to come along at just the right moment to save them from drowning. They nearly tipped the canoe over as they were pulled in sopping wet.

I knew the feeling; it reminded me of the time Em and I had stolen a canoe from someone's backyard in the old town and took it out into the bay. It was a workout trudging through the weeds in the shallow swampy area, but when we got out onto the big lake it was even harder. The water was rough. We tried to keep the boat straight but the wind kept turning the canoe sideways, and we nearly tipped every time a wave hit the side of the boat.

"Steer!" I yelled.

"I don't know how!" she yelled back.

Neither of us had known what we were doing as we tried to get back to shore. But the wind worked against us, sweeping us into the mouth of the bay and into the direct path of the float planes that landed on the hour. As a plane got closer and closer, we stopped paddling and froze. Em looked at me wide-eyed like I knew what to do as the plane came in for a landing, headed straight for us.

"Jump!" I shouted, and we abandoned the canoe on opposite sides, jumping into the freezing water. Treading frantically, we watched it touch the surface and skip like a rock out in front of us, first one ski then the other.

"Grab onto the side," I said as we kicked our legs as fast as we could, using the boat to keep us afloat and help get us to shore. We were almost in the clear, but then Em started screaming out in pain and let go of the boat.

"What happened?" I yelled and swam over to her, still trying to hang on to the boat for fear of it floating out of reach.

"Something bit me!" she cried.

"What do you mean?" I took in a mouthful of water.

"I don't know. Something bit me. I can't swim." She floundered and slapped the water, unable to keep her chin above the surface.

"Just grab the boat and don't let go," I ordered. Somehow, I found the strength to tow Em and the boat on my own as I swam with one arm. I was exhausted when my feet finally touched the bottom, but I pulled us the rest of the way into a bog.

Em dragged her leg behind her as she tried to get to dry ground.

I put her arm around my neck and helped her hobble to a rotted crooked wooden dock, where she sat down and rolled up her pant leg to inspect the damage. The jagged gash oozed a thin stream of blood on the back of her calf and showed clear teeth marks when I cupped my hands in the shallow mud water and poured it over the wound to wash away the blood.

"Must have been a jack," I said. "Those things have ugly fangs." I knew it could only have been a jackfish because every so often my mom would have a variety of fresh fish sitting in the kitchen sink given to her by my auntie, who would also bring her wild meat whenever she came to town. My mom would always say she never liked jack "full of bones." It scared me to look at its gnarly mouth and I'd be relieved when she'd toss it out the living room window to the birds.

"Is it bad?" she asked, afraid to look at it.

"Well, it's gonna leave a nasty scar, but it's not as bad as that leech on your ankle," I said jokingly, making her scream.

"I'm joking, there's nothing on you." I couldn't help but laugh at what a baby she was being.

"It's not funny, Nyla." She sat down and started crying again.

I didn't think it was necessary, but she had gone to the nearest house and asked to use the phone to call her dad to pick her up. I abandoned the canoe upside down in the mud and covered it with weeds. With my shoes muddy and sopping wet, I walked home alone through back alleys to make sure her dad didn't see me on his way down the hill.

I couldn't help but wonder what would have happened if the fish had bitten me instead. Would Em have been able to get us both to shore?

Noah's hand slapped the water hard and snapped me back to the lake when he yelled across the water, making fun of the guys in the canoe. Was he the type of person that would let his friends drown like he did to his hamsters?

Noah was the only one that made it across that day. Everyone hollered and cheered as he flexed his muscles and yelled in victory from the other side.

Em and I slowly drifted apart after Noah came around. She knew Noah and I never cared for each other and eventually stopped trying to make us get along. When she told me Noah thought I was a lesbian because of how jealous I was about the two of them being together, I began to wonder about it myself. All I knew was that I loved Em more than I loved myself. Knowing that they talked about me when I wasn't around made me almost sure she had told Noah about the life-sized poster in my room of a half-naked Courtney Love and a part of me felt like I couldn't trust her with my secrets anymore. Did he know I idolized Kurt Cobain after I saw him break his guitar on stage on live TV at Em's house? Kurt was the only man I truly adored. I didn't know who I loved more, Courtney or Kurt. They were both equally messed up in their own way, which made me feel better about myself. I strived to be like them. I wanted to be in a band but never played an instrument. Except that time when Em's dad bought her a keyboard and we both played around with it for a while until we lost interest, neither of us knowing how to read music. Em could have easily asked her dad to put her in music lessons, but she didn't have the desire. I would have jumped at the chance. Being in a band seemed so limitless; you could get away with anything if you were a rock star. You could be weird, and no one would question you. Em didn't care for grunge; she preferred to listen to dance music, but knowing how much I loved grunge and heavy metal, as a surprise gift one year, she added Nirvana's latest album to her wish list from her dad to give to me.

After my idol died, we tried to reach him through a homemade Ouija board. It didn't work, so I started channelling Kurt's easy and affordable style: flannel, ripped jeans and messy hair. I even thought up a band name and carved the word "stale" into my ankle with a steak knife but the only thing stale was mine and Em's friendship after Noah entered the picture.

By the end of the summer Em seemed to have forgotten all about me. Whenever I called her to see if she wanted to hang out, her phone went to a busy signal. I don't know how many times I pressed redial. I wished I could knock on her door, but by then I wasn't even allowed on her floor after her dad found out I'd been pinching from his pot stash under his mattress.

Then, after not talking for months, she called me up out of the blue.

"Hey Nyla, how's it going? Long time no talk. A few of us are going camping for the weekend at the old cemetery. Wanna come? I know how much you like that kind of stuff."

I was listening but wasn't sold on the idea. "Stuff?"

"You know. Like *morbid* stuff," she teased, reminding me of our word.

"Who's all going?" I asked, already knowing the answer.

"Oh, you know, just me and Noah and one of his friends."

"Oh, I get it. You only want me to go so his friend won't be a third wheel."

"Come on, Nyla. It's not like that. We haven't hung out in forever."

"Where's Kayley? Why isn't she going?"

"She's on vacation with her parents in Meh-hico," she said, trying to sound cool pronouncing the name of the country like that.

"I don't know. I'll think about it."

"Okay, well, we're heading out tonight. You know where we'll be if you change your mind," she said and hung up.

Even if I wanted to go, I didn't know what to pack for camping. The only other time I had gone camping was a time I wanted to forget. My mom's last boyfriend in a string of bad boyfriends lived with what he could fit on his motorcycle. One day he invited us to camp at his site on the beach. We had to walk, and when we got there he had his yellow corn snake hanging off a branch in a nearby dead tree — it looked like a scene out of the Bible.

"He's harmless," he said as it slithered and hung over me. In the morning, when my mom stepped outside of the shared tent to use the outhouse, her boyfriend took the blue-striped pillow out from his sweat-stained pillowcase in our small, musty tent and told me to put my head inside to find a surprise.

I felt I had no choice. I put my head in and there was his snake, coiled in the corner at the bottom. I'm not sure if I imagined it jumping out at me or if it actually did.

The next night my mom scolded me for playing with fire when I accidentally lit a marshmallow on fire at the end of a stick and waved it around to put out the flame.

My mom put on her nicest voice in front of her new "friend." "Nyla, you're going to piss the bed if you play with fire, don't chu know." And they both let out a roar of cruel laughter.

Watching their drunken, sloppy joy at my expense, I wished so bad I didn't have to spend another night in that shared tent with the two of them. Why hadn't she just left me at home alone like she usually did?

My wish came true because as her friend was chewing while laughing, he started to choke on the chicken bone he had hanging out the side of his mouth after he had sucked off the meat like a caveman. At first he tried swigging it down with his beer but spewed the drink back up into the fire and started to gasp for air.

"Are you okay?" my mom asked, but he couldn't talk. He could hardly breathe. He coughed repeatedly and danced around the fire in a panic like he was at a Drum Dance on speed. My mom tried to pat his back, but he hit her hand away. He bent forward and tried to make himself throw up by lodging his finger down his throat, hurling and heaving, but nothing came out except slobber.

"Nyla, don't just stand there!" my mom said, expecting me to know what to do.

Before either of us could do anything, her boyfriend stumbled to his motorcycle and sped away. My mom assumed he went to the hospital and followed on foot. Not wanting to be left behind in the dark alone, I ran to keep up with her. Not once did she look back to see if I was there or not. Thankfully, the hospital wasn't too far. It was dark and cold the second we stepped away from the heat of the fire, but my mom didn't seem to care. She was adamant about making sure he was okay.

If only she gave me one iota of the same kind of attention she gave her boyfriends, my life might have been different.

When we got to the emergency room, he wasn't there. My mom told one of the nurses on call that she was his wife and they let us into a room where he was still coughing away on a gurney.

"Has the doctor come to see you yet?" my mom asked.

He still couldn't talk and just shook his head, making the most horrendous sounds I'd ever heard.

Finally, the doctor came into the room, calm as can be, with a large needle that he jabbed into my mom's soon-to-be-ex boyfriend's arm.

"Try to relax," the doctor said, helping him lie back on the inclined gurney.

"This is going to open your dad's airway," the doctor said to me and I made a grossed-out face.

Then, just like magic, or maybe more like an exorcism, my mom's boyfriend shot straight up and the chunky chicken bone — still fully intact with veins and mucous-covered gristle — escaped his mouth. It hurled across the sterile emergency room, nearly hitting one of the nurses who happened to be walking by. Thankful to be alive and re-evaluating his life choices, the jerk didn't even look at my mom before walking out.

I could hear him down the hallway telling the doctor, "She's not my kid." As he took off in a hurry through the hospital's sliding doors, my mom ran behind him, probably hoping she'd ride off into the sunset with him instead of being stuck with me. She was heartbroken that he left and found a way to blame it on me, but I was just thankful to hear the sound of his motorcycle tearing away.

My mom and I went back to the campsite to pack up what we could. The snake was left behind to wither away in the cold like the sparse leaves on the dry dead tree it hung from.

Needless to say, Em's camping idea was not enticing in the least, but I was curious to see what the old cemetery looked like up close. I'd only ever seen it from across the bay. The haunting white picket fences unevenly covered the hill, jutting out like the backdrop of a scary movie.

Em was right. I did love a good cemetery.

As the evening sunlight poured into my bedroom window the beam of light exposed dust particles in the air, hovering above my bed. I closed one eye and the scene changed. I closed the other eye and saw things in a different way. Were beams of sunlight codes that needed to be solved? What is faster than the speed of light? If it was Superman, then where was he when I needed him?

My hand moved through the beam slowly while I blinked quickly, making my vision dance like a strobe light.

Then I saw it. The scar on my eye. It was a sliver. A jagged squiggly streak on my retina that I could see only for a few seconds when I opened my eye in certain light. The last time my mother hit me, my eye watered for days, and I couldn't see out of it. I didn't know an eyeball could actually hurt or scar until then.

The dust in my room became too much for me to breathe in now that I could actually see it.

I decided to go to the cemetery. I needed to get outside for a bit, and some fresh air and sunlight would do me good even though I didn't feel like doing anything other than lying around in my bed and shutting the world out.

That evening, I made my way to the old cemetery just as the sun was going down. I walked along the highway until I passed the power plant. I ran across the empty highway and climbed down a steep, sliding gravel hill, before I had to go through a short graffiti-filled culvert to get to the ski trail that I hoped would lead me to the cemetery. When I found the ski trail, I knew I was close because I could hear music and laughter in the distance.

Though getting outside was good for me, I still wasn't sure I wanted to be around anyone, so I took a detour and walked around by myself until I decided what to do — I felt like I was walking in circles. I stumbled upon an abandoned black bear den where I had heard a wandering tourist had died the year before after being mauled.

When I got to the cemetery, I tread lightly over the unmarked graves at the bottom of the hill and listened to Em's unmistakable laugh echo off the cliffs through the air around me.

The lake showed signs of an early spring melt, and the water from the snow at the top of the hill was splashing up against the jagged rocks. The hike made me thirsty, but I had forgotten to pack water, so I cupped my hands and took a sip from the small creek that trickled over the rocks next to a small wooden bridge where ice caves formed in the winter, attracting tourists.

When I looked up, I realized the graves weren't just on one level; they were layered up the hill. Surely the runoff from the small waterfall had run through and over long-dead, rotted corpses before finding its way into my own dying youth. The only difference between the dead and me was that at least their spirits had found rest.

Years of spring melt had eroded everything in the water's path, and water had gradually lifted what remained of the bodies from the soil, flooding the graves and exposing bones. Mounds of dirt were broken open to reveal the corners of wood caskets that had once been buried deep. Moss, roots and weeds burst through the earth and entwined with the skeletal remains.

The old cemetery was nearly forgotten. It was a place where loved ones were buried in the time of the tuberculosis epidemic, when only black-and-white photos existed. The new cemetery was on the other side of town, and it was much better taken care of. Bright flowers adorned the wrought iron gate that opened to a winding road with large statues. Coppertown had put off maintaining the old cemetery for far too long and, year after year, the flooding got more out of control. It would be impossible to determine the names of the dead. If it had been any darker, I probably would have been afraid, but I was more fascinated than anything.

After trying to spit out the metallic taste of contaminated grave water from my mouth, I crossed back over the bridge, expecting it to collapse underneath me at any moment. I sucked up my pride and made my way up the steep slope to Em and her friends.

The one tent they had was set up haphazardly, pitched but crooked. Everyone was already more than a few drinks in when I got there. I counted heads. Turns out they found someone to replace me, making me the fifth wheel.

I wanted to turn and leave before they saw me, but it was too late. I was in the clearing by then and they were all sitting around the fire, faced my direction.

"Nyla!" Em said excitedly and jumped up, tipsy.

No one else stood up or waved; they just glanced at each other and then back at the fire again, like they knew something I didn't. I knew how they felt about me. What they thought. I'm sure they questioned why Em was even friends with someone like me.

"Hey. Thought I'd come say hi," I said trying to sound casual like Noah but ending up sounding sheepish.

"Oooooh! I didn't think you were going to come," Em's words were slurred.

"I'm not staying. Just thought I'd hang out for a bit," I lied. I had brought a change of clothes and was already dreading having to make the long walk back home. I sat down next to Em on a small tree stump and they all carried on their conversation without missing a beat. Something about how hilarious it was to watch Noah struggle to pitch the tent.

I feigned laughter while everyone got more intoxicated as the night went on. No one bothered to offer me a drink, but it was just as well. They looked stupid and I didn't want to sink to their level.

When the fire was just about out, one by one they retreated into their tent. Em hadn't been able to hold herself together after ducking behind some bushes to pee. When she came back to the fire her running shoes were sprayed with pee from squatting. You could see where the urine ran down her legs because her ankles were so full of soot from the fire that the stream cut right through it, leaving a trace line and an itch she was too lit to even scratch, though I saw her try. She plopped over onto Noah, who decided to help her into the tent and supposedly "take care of her." After a while, the other couple, whose names I don't care to remember, piled into the tent mumbling something incomprehensible as they held each other up.

I sat outside the tent, listening to them howl drunkenly inside. I didn't wish to be in there with them, but I still felt left out. It was too dark by then; it was the end of the summer and the midnight sun had gone to rest. It wouldn't be so easy to find my way back without a flashlight. So, I sat and stared at the fire slowly dying and tried to figure out what to do.

In some unexplainable way, it felt like the fire was there for me. Like an old friend. It too had been left to burn alone.

A few old pallets sat piled up next to the makeshift firepit. I had always wanted to see what a bonfire looked like up close. I picked up a thin sheet of plywood from the ground beside the pallets. It was surprisingly heavy. When I turned it over, I saw that the underside was coated in sticky wet tar. I could smell the fumes. Someone must have salvaged the wood from the construction site at the dump.

I threw the board into the flickering flame to see what would happen. It instantly caught.

The temptation to make the fire bigger was strong even though it went against my better judgment. I threw a pallet on top of the fire, but it wasn't enough. I threw another one, then another one. I watched, entranced, as the sawdust on the edges of the rough-cut boards caught. Soon the immense heat from the fire forced me to back away.

Gusts of wind coming off the lake seemed to reach out and sweep the fire into an invisible grip. Like a hand playing with a string of beads or a toss of long, fine hair, the wind swirled the flames in all directions.

Even as the flames rose to dangerous heights, I still fed it like a mad scientist adds chemicals to glass jars and watches them explode. I added pallets until there was nothing left to feed to the fire.

The heat from the fire burned my skin, melted my eyelashes and the fine hairs on my face. I stepped back, admiring the fire's threatening beauty. I watched in awe as it danced, taking on a life of its own. It crawled beyond the rocks that could no longer contain it, the heat so intense it burst the smaller rocks open.

Hungry for more fuel to stay alive, the fire crawled towards a small patch of willows. This was just the start of its destruction; it did not stop there.

Snapping out of my trance, I ran to it like a mother trying to stop her child from running into traffic. I tried putting it out with my jacket, but that only fanned the fire higher. It was too late. It had become a wild animal that couldn't be tamed.

I looked over at the tent. I could see the heat starting to melt the thin blue material that Em and her friends were sleeping in. The plastic was shrinking and tightening around the poles like a deflating balloon. I had to wake her.

I ran to the tent and tried to unzip it, but the metal zipper was too hot. I covered my hand with my sleeve and tried again, but the material jammed in the teeth. I ripped off the flimsy tarp that covered the window screens and screamed at them to wake up but no one budged. The wind and fire together ripped the tarp out of my hand and consumed it in one swallow.

I could see them through the screen. They were all still passed out.

"Get up!" I yelled again, but still they didn't move.

How could they still be asleep? They had only just ducked inside, hadn't they? I didn't know the time anymore. Then it hit me. The smoke from the fire had been billowing heavily in their direction since it started. Maybe they had breathed it in.

But then I saw a small movement. Noah was the first to wake up. Disoriented, he began coughing madly before he could even open his eyes. He squinted through the smoke, his eyes filling with tears. He tried to stand up in the tent but hit his head on the plastic cross bar at the top, which he put together wrong earlier that day when all was well. He opened his eyes and saw the flames in front of him.

"What the hell?" he yelled, and I backed away like a coward before he could see me.

He shook Em and tried to open the zipper so they could get out, but it wouldn't budge. He grabbed the screen above and pulled so hard that he looked like the Hulk as he ripped a hole through the top of the tent. He helped Em out, nearly throwing her. Once out, she was useless. She fell onto the ground, coughing and spitting and rolling around. I wanted to help but I couldn't bring myself to move, afraid they'd hate me for what I'd done.

Noah must have shaken the other two awake. I could see him struggling to try and help them make their way up and out of their shared sleeping bag. I watched as the tent started to collapse on them. The plastic material wilted rapidly in the heat of the fire.

I slunk out of sight to the other side of the flames, not knowing what to do. But Noah spotted me beyond the fire and yelled something at me that I couldn't make out over the sound of the crackling trees closing in on us.

The pair broke out of their sleeping bag and out of the tent just before the flames engulfed what was left of the tent and swallowed it up with Noah inside. I had to turn away as he screamed in pain.

I heard sirens from across the bay but couldn't tell if it was their flashing lights or the glow from the fire coming closer. I ran down the cliff and back to the cemetery, tripped over the scattered human bones at my feet that seemed to reach out to try and pull me down with them. I ran as fast as I could past the cemetery and down the steep rocky hill towards the water.

Who would believe me that this was an accident?

Firefighters, paramedics and police in small rubber boats were speeding towards the destruction I left behind. I would have called out. I would have waved my arms in surrender, but I couldn't bring myself to face the consequences. So I kept running.

When I reached the lake, I was at a dead end. Steep cliffs closed me in. I slipped on a slick wet rock and the dark water at my feet looked like the tar underneath the plywood I wished I had never touched. I thought about jumping into the deep and letting myself silently drift until I sank. Instead, I ran back into the cemetery and hid behind one of the only crosses still standing upright. I hid until the crews passed by me on their way up the hill towards the sound of Noah's sporadic shrill screams of pain ... or was it the sound of the trees burning?

Noah. What had I done? Everyone would think this was on purpose. Em would never forgive me. How could I have let things get this out of control?

Had I willed this to happen? Did I do this on purpose? Deep down, had I wanted him to die?

When I was sure no one else was coming to the rescue, I ran back down to the rocky shoreline of the lake. Gripping my lighter, I let it slip out of my hand and into the water like a murder weapon, hoping to get rid of the evidence. The deep water crashed against the jagged rocks and soaked me to my core as I scaled the rock wall, holding onto thorn-covered hanging vines to prevent myself from falling in. I aimed for a private dock in the distance, my only chance of escape. Lights were slowly turning on in houses dotted along the lake as people woke to the rare sound of sirens in their otherwise peaceful neighbourhood on the edge of town. I held on and cringed in silence even when the thick merciless thorns dug deep into the flesh of my palms.

Stumbling onto a back road, I ducked into the trees behind a row of houses where I lay flat on my stomach, hoping no one would find me. I pressed my cheek into the dirt when they sent the dogs to sniff me out. Released from their master's chains in search of my scent — or maybe they were just family dogs tied up in backyards barking and howling at the commotion of the sirens. My heart was beating so fast I was sure the dogs could hear it. The sweat dripping down my face; I was sure they could smell it.

If it wasn't the fear, it was the guilt that had me in its grip, making me almost delirious.

I lay there for hours, unsure of what to do. More and more fire-trucks arrived, parking nearby. They were so close I could smell the exhaust over the smell of smoke. I heard neighbours talking to one another from across their built-up fences.

"It's a bunch of kids up there in the old cemetery."

I lifted my chin off the ground to see the flames reaching higher and higher into the night sky. They were so bright. Brighter than the stars themselves.

The firefighters worked until morning to put the fire out. The dogs never came for me. I slithered away and out of the trees, blending in with society like the snake I had become, hands in my pockets to hide the dried blood from the thorns that had pierced deep into my tar-stained skin.

I crept through backyards and slunk over fences until I reached my apartment building. As usual, my mother wasn't home. I tucked myself into bed where I lay awake, wide-eyed, and wondered if Noah would succumb to his burns like my father had or if he would be able to endure the pain.

Turns out he was stronger than I gave him credit for. He survived. He had been sent by helicopter to the nearest big city in the south for extensive surgery on his face and back. Skin grafts from the back of his thighs were transplanted onto his face. His burns would heal, but his scars would always remain.

No one had seen me standing there, except Noah. They all thought I had left long before the fire got out of control.

Em told me that when Noah woke up from his medically induced coma he blamed me for the fire once his memory flooded back to him. She stuck up for me, telling him he was just imagining things. She told him there was no one to blame. That it was their own fault for leaving the fire unattended. That he was a hero for saving everyone from the burning tent.

But he didn't want to be a hero. Though he had healed, nothing could make him feel better, and no matter how hard she tried, she couldn't convince him otherwise.

"I know what I saw," he told her angrily.

The fact that she defended me caused so much tension between her and Noah that they eventually split ways. He told her we deserved each other.

It probably didn't help that his looks had changed drastically. He would never again look like the male models in her catalogues. I hadn't thought Em to be the shallow type, and she would never admit to it, but I think she lost her attraction to Noah after seeing him burned up the way he was. It had to be at least part of why it was so easy for her to walk away from him.

Em stuck by me. Even knowing my history of starting small fires everywhere, she wouldn't let herself believe that I would have allowed something like that to happen. Instead, she blamed the night on their own drunken carelessness.

"We should have never gone to bed and left the fire unattended," Em said as I sat and listened to her post-breakup story without a word, without a confession. There was only suppressed guilt mixed with my own attempt at self-denial. The fire had brought us closer again for a time.

"It's no one's fault," she told me, almost like she was trying to convince me too.

Once the firefighters completed their investigation, the fire was officially classified as an accident. Just a bunch of crazy kids drinking. A night of careless fun gone wrong. After that, the city finally put money into fixing up the old cemetery and planted new trees at the top of the hill.

Only in this twisted world could I have heard years later that Noah lived in a tent encampment in the middle of a city down south somewhere, homeless and addicted to painkillers.

For that, I take the blame.

~

THREE

Something changed in me that night. I gave in and accepted what my mother told me: I was good for nothing.

I'll never forget the look on her face the day I stood up to her. She was mopping the bathroom floor in the middle of the afternoon during the commercial break of her regular daytime television talk show.

I was always to blame for her obsessive-compulsive disorder. She had to have things just right once the party was over. The countertops couldn't have one crumb. If I left a sock on the floor or didn't replace the toilet paper roll she would lose it, threatening to break every bone in my body. If she didn't have a drink, her irritation would turn into an aggravated cleaning frenzy that she should probably have been medicated for. She was so meticulous that when I did try to help it was never good enough. I was damned if I did and damned if I didn't.

I had walked past the open bathroom door on my way to my bedroom with my head down, trying not to be noticed when she said, "You're so damn lazy, how come you never help me around here?"

I was going to keep walking by and try to ignore her or beg her to forgive me for existing like I usually did, but sometimes that only enraged her more. So this time I thought I'd try something different.

I stopped in my tracks and walked a few steps back to face her. With one foot in the bathroom, I took a good hard look at her. It felt as if I had never really looked at her before. And maybe I hadn't. Come to think of it, I don't remember ever looking into my mother's eyes. I was always too afraid of her.

Seeing my own reflection in the mirror behind her, I also saw for the first time that I was taller than her short and hefty frame. She'd always seemed bigger than me, but it was just her temper that towered over me long after I outgrew her.

She glared at me with her head to the side and opened her mouth to say something, but before she could find more hurtful things to say, I took one long stride towards her, grabbed her by both arms and pushed her against the wall, cornering her between the bathtub and the toilet.

"What are doing? Let go of me!" she screamed and tried to wriggle away, but I was too strong.

"Don't ever talk to me like that again," I said, calm and calculating, pointing my finger so close to her eyeball I thought I might poke it out.

"Let go of me right now you crazy — "

"No!" I screamed and pushed her harder into the wall before she could insult me again.

She looked at me with confusion, and I saw a glimpse of fear in her eyes, which caused me to release my grip on her. Once free, she swung at me but missed. That's when I hastily picked up the bucket full of dirty water, looked her dead in the eyes and dumped the warm, discoloured slop full of clumps of hair and bits of toilet paper over her head. I watched it cascade down her shocked face.

I didn't know whether I should feel sorry for her or burst out into crazed laughter. All I thought then was that she deserved it.

The last drops of mop water dripped off the tip of her nose and into her mouth as she sputtered and sobbed. She lunged at me but slipped in the puddle at her feet and had to use the mop she was still holding to help keep herself from falling into the tub.

I walked into my bedroom and wrestled with the sliding accordion, wishing I had a normal door to slam, as she let out a slew of curse words that I'm sure caused the neighbours to put in yet another complaint. Expecting her to come after me in revenge, I was ready to defend myself again if need be.

Instead I heard the front door slam.

That night I had the sudden urge to throw up and made my way to the washroom. Suddenly I saw myself from above, lying there on the bathroom floor next to the toilet. Sometime later in the night, I woke to the sound of someone rapping on my plastic door only to realize it was me hitting it over and over again. The overwhelming feeling of being outside robbed me of my breath, and I woke up hyperventilating.

My mom was gone for days. I thought I heard her footsteps coming down the hallway and stopping at my door but there was no one there. She was on another one of her binges.

This time though, it wasn't alcohol she ran to. She'd found a new addiction.

It didn't take long for her to become complacent about hiding her new drug of choice — heroin. Soon enough, there wasn't a square inch of our tiny apartment that didn't have a needle hiding in it. I started to find them in the ceramic coffee container or in the flour and sugar containers. Lying atop the soil in the plant pots. Under the couch. Sometimes she didn't care to hide it and left it right out in plain sight on the coffee table. I went into her room one day when she wasn't home and found a spoon with leftover white, crusted powder next to a used needle. I was so sick of seeing it everywhere that I smashed my fist through the cheap drywall of her bedroom right through to the living room.

She didn't even care when she saw the gaping hole. The drugs had made her stop caring about everything, even cleaning.

If it could make someone like her calm then what could the harm be in it, I thought. All alone, I threw on the old mixtape that Em made me and lay on the floor in the middle of the living room, listening to the eclectic sounds of the seventies blasting loudly out of the stereo next to my head, one of the instruments sounding like a stampede of elephants drowning out the constant noise in my mind.

When the song ended, I brought myself over to sit on the stiff, velvet, flower-print couch my mom found at the dumpster in the parking lot of our apartment and hauled in with the help of one of her temporary boyfriends. I grabbed her familiar belt — the one she used to chase me around the house with — and tied it around the top of my arm just like I'd seen in the movies. When my veins started becoming more noticeable, I grabbed the needle. Just as I was about to jab myself with it, I heard someone at the door. I quickly tried to hide the evidence but I had no time; the door wasn't locked and Em let herself in.

"What are you doing?" she yelled and ran over to me, slapping the needle out of my hand. "Are you trying to kill yourself?"

I slid off the couch into a depressed, crumpled mess on the floor.

"Don't you ever knock?" I asked without really caring that she found me in such a state.

She looked at the needle in the middle of the dirty shag rug where it had landed like an arrow stuck straight up instead of in my skin if she had happened to walk in a second later.

"Where'd you get that from, anyway? Honestly, Nyla. Promise me you'll never try that again," Em said, placing her hand on mine.

I nodded slightly to appease her. "What are you doing here anyway?" I hadn't seen Em in over a month; she was too busy with her "extracurricular activities," as her dad like to call them.

"I came to pick up some of my clothes. You know, the green velvet bodysuit I loaned you."

"It's somewhere in my room."

"I see you're listening to my mixtape."

"You come here to take that, too?

"Nyla. Come on," she said as she stood up and reached out her hand to help me up. Stubborn, I stayed sitting on the ground next to the musty couch and crossed my arms. She gave up and strutted off to my room where I could hear her rummaging around for her clothes.

"Where'd you find that gross dirty old needle anyway?" she yelled from the bedroom.

Before I could even answer, she was back in the room and onto a new topic. "Noah's back at school. He's really acting differently. Angry all the time. I guess I'd be, too …" Her voice trailed off.

Not one for any length of awkward silence, she started again, "Anyway, I better get going. My dad catches me here and I'll be grounded again. Promise me you're okay?"

I nodded again, and that was enough for her to let go of any concern she might have had for me as she walked out, leaving me to remember how bad of a listener she'd always been.

I could have sworn I saw her wipe her hands on her jeans and lift her shoulders in a shudder before the door shut behind her.

I kept my promise. Besides, I needed food more than I needed anything else. The fridge had been empty for days. All that was left inside was half a jar of pickles and a bottle of ketchup turned upside down with the lid half open, forming a crusted circle. A few crackers and a packet of noodles sat in the cupboard but having previously gotten sick from eating one too many of them raw, the noodles no longer appealed to me.

I waited until the day after my mom got her income-support money to raid her drawers while she was passed out. I took two out of three small white bags that were hidden in her rolled-up socks. The powder was stuffed into the corner of clear plastic bags that were cut and twist-tied at the top and looked like a teardrop shape.

There was only one place to go with it. Downtown.

I asked the first person I saw standing around smoking outside the Coppertown bar.

"Hey, you know where I can find anything?" He knew what I meant.

He shook his head. "No, but she might." He pointed down the road to the only girl in a group of guys that looked to be only a few years older than me.

I'd seen her around before, always hanging out on the corner downtown, mostly outside the mall harassing strangers as they walked by trying to mind their own business on their way to work.

Carli told everyone she was from Mexico, but really she was from one of the communities further north like me. She kicked it every day on the street in a pair of bright, white running shoes. I still don't know how she kept them so immaculately clean after hanging around grime-filled alleyways day in and day out.

She saw me coming before I walked up to her in the crowd.

"Hey girl, what's up?" she asked as she looked me up and down.

"I got something I need to get rid of," I said in an unnaturally shaky voice.

"Oh yeah?" She chewed her gum heavily on one side of her mouth and tipped her head to the side for me to follow her into the shadows that lined the back alley.

I showed her the stolen goods. She gave me a weird look.

"Where'd you get this?"

"My mom."

"Nice," she laughed.

"How much can I get for it?"

"A couple bills."

"That's it?"

"Hey, you asked."

"Okay, I guess."

"Follow me and stop looking suspicious."

I followed her in silence as she walked briskly, chewing and snapping her gum loudly between her front teeth, over and over. When she crossed the road, she didn't look both ways; she just sort of skip-ran to one side. I thought for a second she might start doing lunges, but it was her way of checking to see if anyone was following us.

She led me to an old, run-down housing complex in the middle of downtown, a few blocks from the pub and up a small hill overlooking the back of a school. I walked in not knowing what to expect.

It looked like my house after one of my mom's parties, and I recognized some familiar faces. Everywhere I looked someone was passed out on the floor, half sitting up or toppled over one another.

Carli walked up to the only person in the place who wasn't in a self-induced coma. He was standing with his back to us in the kitchen, scratching his butt through a pair of ill-fitting dirty grey joggers that hung well below his waist. She greeted him with a half nod.

"That's Junkie John," she whispered behind his back as he led us into a small room underneath the stairs off the kitchen.

"What do you need?" he said in a raspy voice that sounded like he had just woken up.

"Actually, we got something you might want," she said.

Carli gave him one of the bags to inspect. He ripped a small hole in the corner of it with his teeth, dug his long pinky nail into it, and rubbed it on his tooth to make sure he wasn't being ripped off.

In a matter of minutes, he had used the flame from a lighter to melt the powder, which he had put on a bent spoon. When he rolled up his sleeve, I had to look away. His arm was riddled with needle marks and covered in dried blood. He looked for an area of skin that wasn't already broken and stuck the needle in.

When Junkie John was done, he grabbed a random sock off the floor and wiped the blood off his arm.

"Good stuff. How much?" He said with a phlegm-filled snort.

"That depends," she said. It was code for something because he took Carli by the hand and led her up the stairs. "Come on," she whispered to me.

The next thing I knew, the three of us were behind closed doors in a bedroom where someone was passed out on an old, urine-stained mattress. Carli sat on the edge of the bed and Junkie John walked over to her, grabbed a blanket and covered the both of them with it.

"Don't move." He lifted his head from under the thin ratty blanket to warn me.

There was a lot of movement and the sound of moaning. I

wanted to get up leave. I wanted to run right out of there but I also wanted what I came for, so I sat in deep discomfort between the door and wall with my head down looking at my feet and my hands over my ears.

It was over as fast as it began. When Junkie John pulled his pants back up, he said to me, "I like an audience." He threw a twenty-dollar bill at my feet as he walked out the door.

Carli took the rest of the money for herself.

"Where's my gold watch?" my mother screamed in my face as I walked through the front door. The house looked like it had been ransacked after her desperate search to find her stash.

"I don't know what you're talking about," I said, shoving her out of my way on the way to my room.

She ran after me and yelled, "You know exactly what I'm talking about!" She slapped me hard in the face when I turned around to confront her. "Where is it?"

"Where's what?" I yelled back, standing on my tippy toes to tower over her so she wouldn't try to hit me again.

"My gold watch!"

"Gold watch? You don't just want to come right out and say it? Well, I sold it. Are you happy now? Is that what you want to hear?" I watched her face sink in horror at the nerve I had to do such a thing.

"Get out! Get out of my house now!" she raged.

"Fine. I don't want to be here anyway." I stormed to my room, grabbed a few changes of clothes, stuffed them into a plastic grocery bag and left the rest.

There was nothing else I wanted to take with me. No hurt, no pain, no memories. Nothing.

As I left, I looked at my mom one more time. She desperately rooted through the old boxes stacked on top of one another in the hallway, tossing them aside when they turned up void of her fix.

KATŁĮĄ

The world outside that once terrified me now just seemed to laugh at me. I had nowhere to go. The only person I could turn to was someone I didn't want to have anything to do with.

I found Carli standing on the street corner where I first saw her. It was her territory. She could always be found there. Scheming. Hustling.

"Hey, girl, you ready to come and make some real money yet?" she asked, only half-joking. "You know you're a catch," she winked.

Carli had a masculinity about her, and it wasn't just her features. It was the way she walked, the way she carried herself, the way she looked at me.

I forced a smile. "Can I stay at your place for a while? My mom kicked me out."

"Of course she did. You messed with her stash, man. What'd you expect?"

"Yeah, I guess."

"Want me to kick her ass? I can go over there and fuck her up."

I didn't know how to respond. Was she serious?

"No. I'm good."

As horrible as my mother was to me, I didn't wish her ill. I had seen her in a lot of pain once before after being badly beat up by a jealous girl one night. Both her eyes were swollen shut.

"I'm just kidding around," Carli laughed. "My place isn't much but, yeah, I gotcha."

It was only supposed to be temporary. Crash at Carli's until I could figure out what to do next, but one night turned into a week, and a week turned into a month and, soon enough, I'd been there for nearly a year. There were always people coming and going — it wasn't new to me, but it took me a while to catch on that Carli was selling herself. They didn't come right out and ask me, but I could sense that some of the guys that came through Carli's place were wondering about me. Carli would usually protect me if she caught them looking at me.

"Leave her alone," she'd snap. Eventually, whenever they came over I'd just hide in the bathroom until they left.

One night, we got to talking real deep after a few hits of weed from a homemade water bong, and I came right out and asked her, "Why do you do it?"

"Do what?"

"You know. Go to bed with them." I didn't like saying the word sex; it made me feel weird.

"This is a job Nyla. Just like anything else. I'd rather be doing this than working at McDonald's," she said. I didn't believe her. Something in her voice sounded broken.

After a while, I got used to seeing the same guys come around, the regulars. Paul, who was old enough to be my father, was one of them, and he was relentless, always trying to make small talk with me between his visits with Carli.

When he caught me one day mindlessly watching TV in the living room while Carli was in the washroom, he asked, "How's it going?"

"Fine," I said and stared at the TV, wishing he would disappear.

"Why aren't you in school?"

"School?" I looked at him like I forgot what that word was.

"Yeah, school," he laughed.

"I don't need school. There's nothing school can teach me," I said and continued staring at the TV, hoping he would go away. Why was Carli taking so long in there?

"Oh yeah? Then what're you doing hangin' around here?"

"I don't have anywhere else to go." Stop with the questions already, is what I wanted to say.

"You want to make some real money? Some hard-earned money?"

I looked at him with disgust.

"No, I mean an actual job. My boss is looking for a dispatcher over at one of our construction sites on the highway."

"You mean like a *job* job?" I asked.

"Yeah, like a *job* job," he mimicked. "Show up ready for work tomorrow. I'll let 'em know you're coming."

He handed me a piece of paper with scribbled directions on it.

"I'll think about it," I said. There wasn't much to think about. It was an opportunity to make some money and maybe even get my own place.

I showed up at the construction site around midday. I'd only just rolled out of bed and borrowed enough for a one-way cab fare from Carli, not telling her what it was for.

The site was on the side of the dusty highway at the end of a long stretch of dug-up dirt road, fifteen or so minutes out of town by car.

I knocked softly on the door of the shipping container that had the company's logo plastered to the metal siding. "Paul said you were looking for someone to dispatch?" I said to the guy inside. He was wearing a hardhat and standing with his hands on his hips while he looked sideways at a blueprint on the wall.

"We've been expecting you all morning. Here's a radio." He checked to see if it worked by hitting it on the table and tossed it to me when it made a scratchy sound.

"Grab a hard hat. One of the guys out there'll tell you what you need to know. Come to work on time tomorrow."

And, just like that, I had a job.

There was just one problem. I didn't know how I was going to get there and back to Carli's every day. Paul offered to drive me and it felt almost too nice, but it was either that or hitchhike.

After a couple of hours of work I already wanted to quit, but I stuck it out. The desire to have enough money saved up to get my own place outweighed the downsides of the job. Getting yelled at by random drivers with road rage was not something I wanted to get up for every morning, but I did it anyway with a somewhat brighter future in mind. The bugs were horrendous as I stood on the side of the highway holding a sign in the hot sun and the rain. I didn't trust that the radio would help me if a bear or wolf was around, and I looked into the forest behind me every few minutes.

I dragged myself up and out of bed to meet Paul at the gas station to get to work on time each morning that summer. I wish I knew then about workplace harassment and my rights. It wasn't Paul who was bothering me, but his boss. Trying to figure out how to clock in my time at the end of the day was not easy. I sat in front of the sawdust-covered paperwork at his desk with him leaning so close over my shoulder that I could tell he hadn't flossed his teeth in years. I felt uncomfortable so I tried to make light conversation.

"Nice picture," I said as I stared straight ahead at the calendar on the wall. It showed a tall, spindly rock with a hole in the middle of it, sticking out of the water on a deserted beach.

"That's Cabo. I have a vacation house there. Maybe I'll take you there someday if you play your cards right."

I smiled politely but was mad at myself afterwards for not quitting right then and there.

"He gives me the creeps," I yelled over the music in the dingy basement strip club I found myself in as I sat next to Carli in a booth at the side of the stage after work one day. With makeup on, I looked of age in a bar full of random transient out-of-town workers.

"You know on my first day he asked me if I had a boyfriend. Like, within the first hour. I lied and told him I was in a long-distance relationship."

I would have gone on talking but wasn't sure if Carli was even listening. I followed her eyes to find her entranced by the naked dancer grinding on the pole on the small stage in the corner of the bar. Darkened mirrors reflected the woman's body countless times backwards into a spiralling abyss.

"Why did you bring me here of all places, anyway?" I took a sip of my water and looked around at the grubby men, many that I recognized from the work site, still in their work clothes. They talked about meeting up every day after work for a drink, and I watched as they drooled over the latest woman sent in from out of town to dance on stage.

Carli broke her gaze and turned to me when the dancer was done her set and stepped off stage to cover herself in a bright green fuzzy robe.

"You should try dancing," she said as she sipped her rum and coke from a straw. "You could make some real money."

"No, thanks. How much do they pay you anyway, the guys?" I finally asked out of a growing curiosity.

"Depends. A few hundred give or take."

"Wow," I said in surprise. I was hardly making that much in a week.

The next day my boss ran his hand up my thigh while I sat at the computer trying to clock out.

I stood up fast. "Fuck it. This isn't worth it." I grabbed my bag and headed for the door.

"Where you goin'?"

"Find someone else. I'm not your girl."

Paul must have seen me storming out in a fury because he caught up to me on the side of the highway in his truck on my long walk back to town. He was wearing his yellow hard hat and driving one of the company trucks when he rolled down the passenger side window. My adrenaline was pumping too fast to be afraid of any wildlife.

"Hey, where you going?"

"I'm done."

"What do you mean?"

"I quit."

"Why?"

"I just don't want to work there anymore." I didn't need to explain anything to him, and he wouldn't understand anyway.

"Well, get in. I'll drive you back to town. It's about to pour." I would have much rather walked to blow off some steam, but I could see the rain clouds rolling in ahead of me so I jumped in and slammed the door. Dust flew everywhere.

"Why you quittin' already?"

"Just not cut out for this kind of work, I guess." I stared straight ahead angrily, not wanting to talk about it to him of all people.

"I'm heading back to Carli's," I said when he turned off onto the highway that led out of town.

"I know, but I thought maybe we'd go for a little drive."

I didn't want to go for "a little drive" but also didn't feel like I had a choice at that point. Being polite never seemed to work. I wonder now if maybe I'd been more assertive, if I'd demanded to be let out, if things would have been different. I sat quietly in the passenger seat of the grubby truck worrying about what his intentions might be. It wasn't like I could just jump out of a moving vehicle. The road led to a dead end in the summer months when it met the shores of a large lake about sixty miles from town. In the winter months, the lake was used as an ice road for truckers to go to and from a diamond mine in the tundra, where my mother once worked.

I once overheard her telling stories about a poltergeist that haunted the mine. A man had died in his sleep of a massive heart attack and had haunted the camp ever since.

"It thinks I'm his girlfriend," mom had joked with her friends in the late hours while I listened from my room. "He rubs my back sometimes when I'm working alone in the kitchen. Plays with my hair. I look like her, the miners say. Like his girlfriend." She said that the men in the camp weren't so lucky, that they'd been tormented by the ghost.

"You ever been out this way? To the end of the road?" Paul asked.

I shook my head. I tried not to let him see that I was uneasy. Except for the hum of the engine, the cab of the truck was so quiet that I almost worried he could hear my thoughts.

"So, do you have a family?" I asked, hoping he would say yes.

"No. No family. Never really settled down."

My mother had never warned me about getting in vehicles with strangers. Even if she had, would I have listened? I trusted Paul enough to give me a ride to work and back for a short time, but that didn't mean I knew him. All I really knew about him in that moment was that he loved to run over ptarmigan and eat roadkill.

"When they get caught up in my truck tires, it just makes it easier to pluck 'em. I like the hearts and feet the best," his small talk was making me feel more uneasy.

I just pursed my lips and nodded my head in a half smile, afraid I might have shown the disgust on my face.

He pulled the truck to a slow stop once we reached the end of the road. A gate submersed in water with a signpost read the obvious, "Road Closed." He shut the engine off and turned towards me, his arm outstretched on the back of the truck's bucket seats. I looked down at the pile of garbage at my feet, mostly fast-food wrappers and dirty travel mugs with the company logo sprawled across the handle. When he started playing with my hair, I moved closer to the door.

"What's the matter? You don't have to be shy," he said slyly.

"I'm ready to go back now." There was no question that he knew I didn't want to be there. That's when I knew he wasn't going to bring me back without getting his way.

I wanted to run, but where could I go? We were an hour's drive out of town. I only had two options: try to fight him off even though he outweighed me threefold or let him get it over and done with.

I had never seen a wolf up close before.

Once I thought I saw a pack of them when I was walking back into town on the highway after a day at the beach with Em in late summer. They started howling in the distance when the sun went down. I walked fast, looking far down the road. Then I saw them out of the corner of my eye, to my left. In between the trees. They were hovering over a small animal carcass, scavenging what was left of their kill. One looked up at me with blood all over its face and a hunger in its eyes. I ran further down the road, then stopped. Unafraid. I looked back over my shoulder at the mysterious pack, but they were already gone, leaving me to think that maybe I imagined them.

This wolf, though, was as real as can be. On all fours, he was as high as the hood of Paul's F-150. The lone wolf stalked across the road in front of the truck. I never took my eyes off him, thankful for the distraction.

When it was over, Paul placed a hundred-dollar bill on the dash in front of me and drove me back to town. His whistle cut through the silence like a knife as he tapped to the beat of the music on his steering wheel like nothing had happened.

For days afterwards I was afraid I might be pregnant so I didn't eat. Maybe a baby wouldn't have a chance to grow if I didn't eat. It wasn't that difficult to fast. There was never any food in Carli's fridge except for random produce, like mushrooms, which she fried up and covered in melted cheese.

Carli's fridge had been leaking for days but it didn't occur to her to call the landlord and ask him to come and fix it. She just put a towel underneath the door to catch the drips that pooled and flooded over every few days. The clear vegetable drawer had a stale onion lazily wrapped in plastic and one dried-out garlic clove; flakes of its papery skin littered the bottom of the bin. The fruit drawer was filled with a plastic net bag of mouldy and shrunken mandarin oranges that had been sitting there since Christmas, green and white and nearly hollowed out. The rest of her fridge was filled with expired condiments and half a bottle of homemade wine she'd stolen from one of her clients.

The wine was from the night she tried to seduce me. In an effort to be fancy, she'd lit candles and opened the bottle. Neither of us liked the taste of wine, but we drank it anyway. Not one to drink, I found that it helped me forget about Paul. I don't know how I found myself in Carli's bedroom, but I vaguely remember her trying to kiss me. I had the spins so bad that I threw up over the side of her bed, which must have stopped her from trying to put the moves on me because all I remember after that is passing out and waking up late the next day. I was terrified that the nausea was from morning sickness, but it turned out to be a killer hangover that lasted three days.

"A nice hot bath might make you feel better," Carli said when she came into the room and saw how deathly ill I still looked days later. I had no energy or desire to move. She must have put a garbage can next to the bed just in case I vomited again. At least I had someone taking care of me, I thought. I took her up on the offer after she drew the water for me. Come to think of it my mom had never run the bath for me. I had never had a bath before then that I can remember. Once I was in Carli's tub, the warm water helped me feel better. The water seemed to be the only thing that could take me out of myself and my racing thoughts, even if only temporarily. The tub had no plug, so Carli used a facecloth to stuff the drain. When the water eventually turned cold, I ran fresh water as hot as I could stand it, until my feet tingled from the heat directly under the tap. I looked at my thighs and measured them against the size of the bathtub. Measured the height of them at the water level. I tried not to focus on the porcelain, stained yellow from the years of built-up scum that had probably never been scrubbed clean. I sunk low enough so that only my mouth and nose were above water and felt the silkiness of my hair underwater.

I stayed in the tub until the water turned cold a second time. I pulled gently on the cloth and the water slowly drained. I stayed until the tub was completely empty and I was shivering. The candle Carli had left on the rim of the bathtub flickered wildly in the shadows beside my head, matching my trembling. Carli had left the bathroom door open a crack, and I couldn't help but think that she might have been spying on me.

I didn't want to look at myself in the mirror when I got out of the tub. I was withering away; my stomach was sunk inwards. I had never been skinny, but the person in the mirror was unmistakably thin. My stomach endlessly rumbled, but I ignored it. I didn't want to let what happened to me define me, but the truth was my body didn't feel like my own anymore.

I tried not to think about what happened in Paul's truck. I tried to focus on anything but the way I felt.

I didn't want to feel anymore. I counted the days on the calendar, hoping my period would come on time. Wishing for those familiar uncomfortable cramps to kick in.

Willing to try anything to get my mind off the rape, I took Carli up on her incessant requests for me to meet her at a random party she was going to. Knowing there'd be alcohol to numb the pain. I found myself missing Em and the friendship we once had. I wondered what she would have thought of Carli. I wondered if she would have cared about what happened to me.

When I got there, it turned out it wasn't actually a party in the way I assumed a party would be. It was just Carli and a handful of older men who looked related. I wanted to turn and leave as soon as I got there. I pulled Carli into the bathroom and asked her why she invited me.

"This isn't a party, Carli. What the hell?"

"I know. I know," she apologized without fully admitting she'd been lying to me. I felt tricked. Lured into going someplace she knew I would never have agreed to go. "One of them owns a restaurant and the corner store downtown. They're harmless."

"And?" As if I cared who they were and what they did.

"They've got money to spend," she answered. Her eyes glossed over; she was already high and seemed carefree.

"Besides, you're here now so why not just chill?"

I wanted what she was on. I walked back into the living room where one of the men tightly rolled up a red fifty-dollar bill and handed it to me as soon as I sat down on the partially collapsed black leather couch. It was so worn, I had to either sit on the very edge or sit back and disappear into it. I did the latter. Maybe the couch would swallow me whole. Up until that point I hadn't tried drugs other than sneaking a taste from the heap of cocaine on Carli's coffee table when she went to the washroom. I dabbed it on one of my canines, the same way I'd seen Junkie John do it.

I watched Carli lean in and snort a thin white line up her nose with her own rolled up bill. Everyone looked at me. It was my turn. I leaned over and snorted the thick clumpy line of powder. Seconds later, my eyes started to water. I sat back and waited for a feeling, but I didn't feel anything. Not right away, anyway. While I didn't feel high, I also didn't feel low anymore. I didn't feel anything. I was numb.

Maybe that was the point. I became a mere observer. Like I was outside of my body. Maybe that was why mom used. What was she trying to get away from?

I didn't want to think of her. Why was she here with me? I didn't want to feel sorry for her, not for one second, so I leaned in and took another hit.

The next thing I knew, I was in a dark bedroom, naked and lying on the bed in front of one of the younger-looking men, who had to be in his late twenties. He stood over me at the end of the bed watching me lie there before getting on top of me. Maybe he wanted to be with me, I thought. Maybe he wanted to take care of me.

It was a lie I told myself. He was gone by the time I had gotten dressed.

I don't remember anything after that.

I had already been bought and paid for — I walked right into the snare that Carli had set. Why had she turned on me? I thought she was protecting me from her clients, but she was only protecting herself. She hadn't wanted me to take away her clients, so she found me new ones.

I don't remember how I got back to Carli's, but I know I was alone. The first thing I did was strip down and throw everything I wore in the wash along with the pile of clothes that were lying on the floor in front of the front-facing loader. Little did I know that Carli's cat, a street rescue named Kitty, had been sleeping in the pile of clothes.

I was so out of it that it took me a while to figure out something wasn't right. I heard a clunking sound every time the washer spun. I assumed it was shoes but when the thumping became unbearable, I looked through the window in the front loader to see what it was.

"No!" I yelled when I saw a furry paw. I went to open it but it was on rinse lock. So I scrambled to climb up and over the washer to reach the large plug and yanked it out of the wall so fast it sparked. To my relief, the washer made a clicking sound and unlocked. Kitty lay atop the mix of clothing all frazzled and wet. I picked him up and tried to hold him, but he wriggled free after he tried to bite me. He walked sideways at my feet, trying to rid his coat of water and fell a few times until he plopped down on the floor and breathed heavily, exhausted and dizzy.

A few days later, Carli complained that Kitty was acting weird. She wasn't wrong; he wasn't the same. For days, he was constantly jumping off the walls and meowing aggressively at nothing in particular or walking around with his back arched and his fur sticking up. I never did tell her what happened. She would have probably thought I did it on purpose to get back at her for pimping me out.

For a long time I accepted that being used and abused might be all I would ever amount to. Maybe life just wasn't fair to people like me. I didn't think much of my future. I self-medicated with whatever I could get my hands on. I was always drunk or high. I would pass out at parties and wake up to find Carli's hand down my pants. I would groan and try to roll over and push her away, but I was too intoxicated to stop her. I found myself in dingy motels with much older men. It got to the point that I would take anything, even pocket change, to get another hit.

Soon enough, I started being turned away by the men who had first got me high. Over time I learned that they were all a part of a sexual exploitation ring in town that targeted young, vulnerable girls like me. Even the sloppy-looking old men didn't want me. They seemed to be a family. It was clear that they were not from the North and they sporadically used words like "washed up" to describe me when they spoke to one another in their language. How could they be sick of the sight of me when this was what they had a hand in turning me into?

I demanded they care about me. I went to them time and again at their places of work, hoping I'd get some sense of self-respect back, but it was always the same. I would only feel more awful for expecting dignity from the people who had taken it away from me.

My need for a decent meal and a fix led me to the only person I could think of who might give me some money for a small favour — an old short bald customer who walked with a shuffle. It was the middle of the day when I knocked on his motel door; I put my finger over the peep hole so he couldn't see that it was me. He must have had a dozen bolt locks to hide his unlawful deeds from the world. His long-term motel room was cluttered. When he opened the door it must have formed a wind tunnel because a strong breeze gusted in through the small, blurry, half-open window above the noisy street below, blowing the edges of the posters of fountains and cherry blossoms. A few paper coin rolls fell off his nightstand, landing next to a small black cash box.

As I half expected, he didn't want anything from me either.

"Not today," he said and tried to shut the door in my face. But I jammed my foot in the door to stop him from slamming it.

"Wait. I just need a couple bucks," I said.

"You're dirty. You need to clean yourself up."

He had no right to judge me but at the time I believed him. I learned later that he was a pedophile videotaping young girls without us knowing. I'm sure he'd already sold footage of me in the underground market before there was such thing as the dark web. I told myself I didn't care.

He handed me some change from his cash box and told me to come back another time. After that, he stopped opening the door for me. A few weeks later, Carli told me that some of the girls on the street found out about his hidden video camera. They broke into his room, beat him up, stole his lockbox and burned the tapes. I guess a small part of me still cared, because I had a slight twinge of hope that any videos of me were in the burn pile.

My aunt had once come to town while I was still living with my mother. She was undergoing an operation and had to stay with us for a while. She was just as bad as my mother. They sat day drinking together, cackling until the laughing turned to arguing over something that happened in the past. My aunt's thin, frizzy hair looked like it had never been brushed. She wore the same clothes every day, and when she spoke, she repeated herself over and over. She even talked to the bugs that crawled around in our utensil drawer. On her last day with us I hadn't wanted to hug her because she smelled terrible, but she pulled me in. When she opened her mouth, all I could see was rotten teeth. I had to turn away from the stench of her breath and hold my own breath. She saw the disgust on my face. Later that night she came into my room thinking I was asleep and whispered from the doorway, "I give you my curse."

Shortly after she left, I started noticing that I had bad breath. Her smell had rubbed off on me somehow. I tried everything to get rid of the stench. I didn't have gum or mints or mouthwash, so I brushed my teeth vigorously throughout the day until my gums receded and the bristles on the toothbrush bent over onto each side like the part down the middle of my hair. Then the smell moved to my armpits. No matter how much I scrubbed, the body odour still lingered. Over the years I managed to keep it somewhat under control, but it flares up again every so often. Usually whenever I'm around certain people. In hindsight, I think of it as an animalistic defence mechanism. Maybe my aunt was doing me a favour. Maybe she cursed me for my own good to rid me of the people who shouldn't be in my life.

～

"You can't just kick me out. Where am I supposed to go?" I begged Carli to let me stay, but even she was starting to get tired of having me around.

"You don't help out. You don't pay rent. You're a mess."

I wasn't holding back anymore and let her have it. "Don't try to act like you're such a saviour. You're a wannabe pimp! You never cared about me!" I yelled.

"You know what, Nyla, you can pack your shit and get out. Look at yourself. You look like shit. You better be gone by the time I get back!" She slammed the door on her way out.

She wasn't wrong. There was no hiding it — I was at my lowest. But I didn't care about my appearance.

I sat with my feet pressed up against the heavy glass coffee table, the only nice thing Carli owned in her half of the rented duplex. It had been left behind by the previous tenants.

Kitty curled up beside me purring, but I didn't want to pet him. I pushed him off the couch knowing he'd land on his feet just fine. Even though he was sketched out half the time, he was a pretty cat — besides missing a piece of his ear from getting into a scrap with another cat in the back alley.

I looked between my toes at the leftover crumbs of cocaine on the table. One more hit, then I'd leave.

I hadn't a clue where I was going.

I gathered up what I could of the bits of hard powder, crushed them up finer and did a line. Then I lit one of the messy candles and watched as the wax oozed onto the glass table. Countless times I'd fiddled with that candle as Carli and I sat and watched movies in the middle of the day with nothing else to do. When the candle was pliable, I would tip it just enough to let the wax drip onto my fingertips, the rest of it spilling and eventually turning to a hardened puddle on the glass. It was difficult to scrape off once hardened because the wax turned into sticky flakes, but Carli didn't care. She was so messy that I don't think she even knew where the garbage can was in her own house. I looked around at the crumpled fast-food wrappers and soggy cardboard cups half filled with melted ice water. Or half empty, depending on which way you looked at it.

I took another hit and lay back on the couch, staring up at the ceiling like I've done ever since I can remember. What would I do now? Where would I go? I struggled with the thought of being homeless.

I didn't have enough money to even make it to the end of the week. I wouldn't make it very far on foot either, with the bottom of my shoes worn right down to the sole. I had last borrowed a pair of Carli's old bulky runners; thankfully we had the same size feet. Before that, Em often gave me her hand-me-downs. I'd never had a brand-new pair of shoes — well, ones that were bought and paid for anyway. Come to think of it, my mom never really bought me anything.

The one time she brought me to the department store, she took a look at my ratty old shoes and said, "You need a new pair of shoes. I don't want anyone thinking you're homeless."

She got me to try on a pair of black hiking boots. "Walk around in them for a bit to make sure they fit," she ordered.

I walked up and down the aisle, only able to take baby steps because the shoes were tied together with a thick black elastic.

"Okay, good enough."

She waved me back over to where she was kneeling on the ground in the middle of the aisle after helping me tie the laces, which were more like laces on ice skates than hikers. She ripped the tag off and bit the elastic with her back teeth until it broke.

"Meet me outside. I've got a few more things to get," she said as she tucked away my old shoes on one of the lower shelves behind a pair of high heels.

"But — "

"Just do it, Nyla," she said angrily between her teeth. She pinched the back of my arm and wrenched it violently. "And stop acting suspicious."

I walked slowly past the busy cashiers with my head down, trying not to make eye contact. I expected the alarms to go off when I walked through the doors, so much so that I stopped on my way out and waited for a few seconds but nothing happened. So I walked out and shuffled my feet in my new shoes while waiting for Mom beside the garbage can outside the sliding doors, too afraid of getting caught to look back.

My mom would steal groceries, makeup, nail polish, even mattresses when people were moving. She stole dishes from fancy restaurants, shoving them into her purse when no one was looking. She even stole a pair of expensive headphones equipped with an alarm tag. It was part of why we had so much stuff crammed into the apartment.

Listing all the things my mom stole, I fell into a deep sleep as if counting sheep. I dreamt I was a young girl again walking out of the department store. This time the store alarm went off, and I froze in fear as the security guards came for me. Just as they lunged towards me, I was jarred awake by the demanding sound of the smoke alarm. In a daze, I looked around to see heavy curls of flames circling the carpet.

I jumped up.

The candle. I forgot to put it out.

The entire blob of wax had slumped over with the wick still lit. Fuelled by the garbage and dried-up alcohol on the table, the flames had travelled and washed over the wall like waves and were crawling across the ceiling above me. It was too late for a fire extinguisher.

I ran through the flames to the front door, but then I remembered Kitty.

"Kitty. Kitty!" I called out for him. Through the smoke, I saw him hiding under the couch. "Come on. Come here, Kitty."

He never did come when he was called, even at the best of times, but this time he was too terrified to move.

I saw the fire reflected in his wide cat eyes as he meowed loudly. I cornered him before he could run away and stuffed him up under my sweater. He squirmed and scratched me as I ran for the door. I tripped and fell, hitting my head on the side of the kitchen counter on the way out. It must have knocked me out for a second, because when Kitty reached up and scratched my neck, trying to escape from the madness, I came to and held onto him tighter. We crawled beneath the smoke until we made it out safely.

I thought I left it in the past, but the fire had followed me.

From the street, I saw the sprinklers turn on, flooding everything Carli owned.

From what I can recall, I sat curled up in a blanket on the side of the road next to the ambulance moments later. After the fire was under control and declared an accident, I heard the firefighters say the place would be salvageable after some major repairs. The majority of the damage was from the smoke.

From what I heard on the streets later, Carli was evicted and moved back to her home community further north to live with her family. Not to Mexico, like she wanted everyone to believe.

As for Kitty and me, we became homeless strays once again.

~

FOUR

I had a routine. I would get drunk at sketchy bars with my fake ID and go home with random strangers. Some call it promiscuity; I call it survival. By that point I had resorted to sleeping in stairwells on the nights I could not find a bed. The shelters didn't take women without children, and I didn't look like a child anymore, but I didn't want to access the youth shelter because I knew they'd try to reunite me with my mother. I was falling through the cracks in the system and was vulnerable to men who preyed on girls like me. Men like Mike who watched me access the food bank from across the street. He must have been watching and listening for some time because he knew my name. He sat in his car in the parking lot outside the church where they gave out free lunch daily. I felt his eyes on me but never let him know I knew he was staring at me, until one day he approached me and offered cigarettes and booze.

"I thought you'd never ask," I said and got in his car. We drove around town aimlessly for a while, and he asked me questions about what I believed in. If I meditated or prayed to a higher power. Why was he so interested in what I thought about life and death?

"I don't know if there even is anything to believe in," I said honestly.

He wasn't a bad-looking guy but he was way older than me. He looked to be in his mid-thirties. Later that night, he drove me through the locked gates of an abandoned copper mine where he worked as the night shift security guard. I wasn't supposed to be there. He told me proudly that he was responsible for monitoring the grounds to make sure no trespassers came around. I really didn't care what he did.

"What happened to your nose? Did you break it?" he asked.

"A long time ago." The bridge of my nose had a bump in it and wasn't quite straight. I hadn't thought it was that noticeable until he pointed it out.

Feeling self-conscious, I tried to mimic his uncouthness. "So, you just sit here all night and do nothing?"

He laughed. "Let's go for a walk."

The last thing I wanted was to go for a walk when all I really needed was a warm place to crash and something to eat, but I went along anyway.

We walked through an open field leading to the rocks that bordered the big lake, stepping over old rusty mining equipment along the way. We climbed the rocks until we found a flat spot and sat looking out at the lake. Behind us, Coppertown was sound asleep, but the midnight sun was still high in the sky. We sipped a mickey of vodka he had tucked in his back pocket. I took a big swig and shifted uncomfortably on the cold, hard rock. It was just my luck that I'd find myself far away from a washroom. I was on my dreadful period and couldn't afford pads, so I had rolled up a thick wad of toilet paper and stuffed it in my underwear. I could feel the blood working its way onto my jeans, having soaked through the toilet paper I had forgotten to change out. Not everyone wanted sex, some just wanted comfort, and I hoped Mike was like that.

But then he said, "Drink up," and tilted the bottle higher to pour the alcohol into my mouth faster.

"Hey. Take it easy," I said and wiped away the alcohol that had dripped down my chin with the sleeve of my sweater.

"You know if you scream out here no one can hear you," he taunted me as he stood up in front of me and started unzipping his jeans.

"You're supposed to pay me first. That's how it works," I said.

"Pay you?" he laughed. "Nah. I'll just take it for free." He grabbed me and slammed me down hard on the rocks on my back.

"I'm on my period," I blurted, hoping that would change his mind.

"I don't care," he laughed, further disregarding any sanctity I had left.

He tried straddling me, but I pushed him off with my legs.

"Hey, be nice."

"I wanna go back!" I yelled adamantly.

Just then his radio went off. "Mike, come in. Mike."

He looked at his watch. "Holy shit, I didn't realize the time." He picked up the mickey off the ground and downed the rest of it in one shot, then said, "You better not say a word to anyone about this. I know where to find you."

He left me alone in the wild.

I stood up and felt a rush of blood come out.

The chances of being mauled to death by an animal and never being found were high, but not higher than being raped or murdered out there in the bush. If I disappeared would anyone know or care to come looking for me? I tied my sweater around my waist and started climbing over the rocks in a different direction than Mike had gone.

I quickly got lost and started to run when I found myself next to a swampy marshland that reeked like rotten eggs. Then I heard the low hum of music. Was I hearing things?

I stopped and listened for a long time. Sure enough, it was the sound of a guitar blaring off in the distance somewhere. Following the sound, I crossed over endless rocks and tree roots until I could once again see the Coppertown skyline. The growing sound of Led Zeppelin started to meld with loud drunken voices yelling over the music. I stumbled into a bush party. There must have been at least a hundred people partying on the rocks that night, and just as I got there the party was being busted by the police on foot patrol. I ran towards some bushes to hide.

That's when I met Alex. He had a bottle of Jack Daniels tucked away in the inside pocket of his leather jacket.

"Sip?" he offered. I took it graciously and we squatted together behind the bushes until the cops left. Only a few of us didn't get caught, and I naturally joined the partygoers and drank with them until our voices were haggard and we could no longer speak in full sentences.

I crashed at Alex's place that night — or day, I should say, because by the time we made it to his parents' basement it was almost noon. Alex was a few years older than me, and I soon found out he was a mama's boy. His mom would pick up after him and cook him dinner every night.

I surfed his couch for the next few days before eventually wearing out my welcome when his girlfriend found out. Imogine wasn't very pretty but she was confident; there was something about her that radiated when she walked into the room or maybe it was just her colourful clothes.

"Oh, you must be here to help clean," she said, looking down on me from the bottom step of Alex's basement.

"Yeah, sure," I said.

I figured Imogine must have complained to Alex's mom about me staying there because the next day his mom came down and said, "It's probably best you leave, Nyla. You've been here for some time now. I'm sure your parents are expecting you back at some point."

She had a caring, motherly tone to her voice. Alex was her pride and joy. It explained how he was allowed to do whatever he wanted, to have friends over at all hours drinking and smoking up in the basement. She was a classic enabler. He could do no wrong.

I could have pleaded to stay. Told her my situation, that I had nowhere to go. She might have felt sorry for me and let me stay.

For a moment, I thought about it. But then I grabbed my things and walked out into the cold. To make matters worse, I slipped and fell in the driveway. I got up, dusted myself off and made my way downtown.

Alex had his own slice of heaven, but that life wasn't meant for me. I had to take the hard road. I had no choice.

~

I spent my days wandering around town, fake laughing on the street with people I didn't know, panhandling change on Carli's old corner. Every night, I found myself back at the bar trying to seduce random out-of-towners who didn't know my small-town reputation. It was an easy place to get picked up, and it wasn't long before I found myself at a top-end hotel in the middle of downtown with a red-headed tourist.

He brought me up to his room for a few drinks after the bar closed. I was so tired, having not slept in days, and the bed looked so comfortable that I couldn't resist lying down. He seemed shy, so I felt safe enough to close my eyes if only for a minute. But I learned that looks can be deceiving.

"Get off me!" I yelled as I woke up. I didn't know how long I was out for.

I managed to push him away from me and jumped off the bed, grabbed my purse and headed for the door.

His beady, black, emotionless eyes followed me out and down the long empty hallway from the doorway of his hotel room.

"Where you going?" he called out after me.

"Don't follow me!" I yelled as I made it to the elevator doors and pressed the button repeatedly while he walked quickly towards me.

"Wait!" he yelled, but the elevator closed before the freckle-faced stalker could jam the sliding metal doors. When I got to the lobby, he flew out the stairwell doors.

"Call the police!" He slammed his fist down on the counter in front of the night receptionist.

"Yes, call the police," I said angrily.

"She tried to steal from me," he pointed at me.

"What? Are you kidding me?" I couldn't believe he had the audacity to lie.

I made my way towards the glass doors of the lobby, leading into the night.

"Excuse me, ma'am. I can't let you leave," the security guard said as he stepped in front of the door to block my path. The woman behind the counter must have pressed a button to lock the door because I heard it click.

"What do you mean I can't leave? You can't lock me in!" I barged past the guard and rattled the door. "I didn't do anything!" I cried. "He did!"

I looked over at the smug redhead as he stood with his head held high and his arms crossed next to the hotel clerk's desk and said, "We'll let the police decide that when they get here."

As enraged as I was, I tried to play it cool. "All right, fine. I'll wait for the police." I threw my hands up in surrender and plopped down on the fancy leather couch in the middle of the lobby. Maybe I'd finally have a good night's sleep in a jail cell without anyone bothering me.

He held his chin up in the air in front of me. He was so angry that his face flushed until it matched the colour of his hair.

As we waited for the police to show up, the sounds of soft piano music played through the speaker system and made time stand still. In the reflection of the glass doors, I saw how dishevelled I looked. It would be my word against his.

When the police got there, they immediately escorted me to their car and let the tourist walk free, believing his side of the story without question.

"How am I in trouble? I didn't do anything wrong!"

I fought back as they tried to forcefully put my hands behind my back and shove me into the back seat. I slipped out of their grip just long enough to give the redhead the middle finger.

That's when the female officer grabbed my finger and pulled it back so hard, it snapped. I jerked it away in pain and they managed to wrestle me into the car. During the drive, I yelled at them and called them every swear word I knew.

"Be quiet back there or we'll have to hose you down to cool you off," the male cop said seriously.

"Do you have anywhere to go?" the female officer asked after I ran out of profanities.

I didn't answer.

"If not, we'll have to put you in a cell for the night."

"Just drop me off up the hill by the school," I said. I put my head back on the seat in defeat and held my finger tightly to stop it from throbbing.

There was really only one place I could crash for the night, but it was far from where I wanted to be. At least it was somewhere out of the cold without having to resort to the stairwells or the shelter that probably had no room for me anyway.

The door was never locked at Junkie John's. There were always people coming and going. When I got inside, I thought I saw Junkie John passed out on the couch. But when I got closer, I knew it couldn't be him because the guy's arms were clean. I couldn't tell if the guy was sleeping or not because he lay there with sunglasses on. It creeped me out, but when I heard him snoring, I let my guard down.

I slid down the living room wall and sat at the end of the couch in the corner, hoping no one would bother me there. I soon fell asleep curled up with my head on my sweater. It had become my pillow to separate me somewhat from the foul carpets I found myself sleeping on more often than not. The house was oddly quiet, but I still stirred awake several times through the night. As my eyes adjusted I looked around in the dark to see an old couple camped out on top of a sleeping bag in the far corner of the living room while rap music droned from somewhere upstairs on repeat. The steady rhythm of it soothed me.

"Here." The guy with the sunglasses offered me a glass of warm tap water the next morning from a glass covered in smeared fingerprints.

I could see that he was older than me, but not by much. He had a sly look about him, but it suited him. He had one of those distasteful triangle-shaped beards, the kind that reminded me of the devil. If he were an animal, he'd be an eagle for sure.

"What's a beautiful girl like you doing here?" he asked.

"My mom kicked me out."

"Oh yeah. What kind of mom would do that?"

I took another sip of the murky water, looking at the bottom of the glass to see if he might have tried to drug me.

"What happened to your finger?" he asked when he saw me trying to move it and cringe.

I gave him a sad, broken, swollen middle finger. He laughed.

"I've got a place across town if you need somewhere to crash for a bit."

"What are you doing crashing here then?" I asked.

"Sometimes this shit gets the best of me, you know. Life's hard, man."

I nodded but I couldn't relate. At least he had a place to live.

"Where's your stuff?"

"My stuff?"

"You know. Your clothes and shit."

"My mom's." I lifted the collar of my shirt and smelled myself, trying to hide my embarrassment. I'd been wearing the same rags for so long I couldn't remember the last time I had clean clothes. The only time I changed was when it was absolutely necessary. I'd go to the Goodwill and scour the donation bins until I found something that fit without the workers noticing. Technically, it wasn't stealing; after all, it was supposed to be for those who couldn't afford to buy new things.

"Well, then, let's go get it."

"I don't know. She'll freak out."

"And?"

"All right, yeah. I guess." It had been so long since I'd seen her that I wondered if she even lived at the apartment anymore.

Clayton was his name, and he chain-smoked all the way to my

mom's apartment while I shivered and breathed out puffs of cold morning air. Winter felt never-ending.

I peered in through the living room window on the hill to see if my mother was home. The lights were all out and the curtains were drawn, which didn't necessarily mean she wasn't home. It just meant she was probably hungover.

I tapped on the window and waited. A few minutes later, she startled me when she pulled back a corner of the curtain and stared out with one eye suspiciously. It felt like a lifetime since I saw her face.

"What do you want?" Her raspy, angry voice sounded muffled through the thin dirty window.

"She wants her shit," Clayton stepped in front of me and stomped out his cigarette on the ground abusively.

"Well, she can't have it. I threw it out. And who the hell are you?"

"Forget it. Let's go." I said and grabbed for Clayton's hand to drag him away. But before I could, he bent over and pulled his pants down to moon her, then lost his balance and fell halfway down the hill on his bare butt in the same spot Em fell years ago.

"Sicko!" My mother yelled out after us as we ran away laughing.

"Why are you being so nice to me anyways?" I asked when we got to his bachelor apartment. He hadn't even seemed to care when I bummed cigarette after cigarette off him.

"You can't be on the streets. I know girls like you found in back alleys who never wake up." His words had conviction. He said it like he meant it.

He said it like he missed someone.

~

FIVE

Clayton and I just clicked. He made me laugh every chance he could. He even shaved off his beard when I told him it scratched me. He shared everything with me. Gave me what was his, including things I could care less about having, like gonorrhea.

I started experiencing a terrible smell down below, to the point that I couldn't take it anymore and went to the walk-in clinic. When I told Clayton the news, he was surprisingly calm about it.

"Why don't I have symptoms, then?"

"It doesn't show up in guys as much."

"At least it's curable," he said, trying to make me feel better.

Clayton's place was actually a transition house and shelter for older youth. It was the first apartment building built in Coppertown, and it was squished between an old, abandoned arena and a park once named after an explorer. The building was so old it was sinking back into the earth and should have been condemned and torn down. Outside his door there was always a commotion. The caretakers didn't care if the residents killed each other. When the caretakers got money from the government to fix up the building they put a few coats of paint on the outside, planted a flower bed, and posted job ads in the hallway, but they couldn't cover up the smell of black mould in the insulation. A single mother lived above us, and all night long her baby cried and cried. There were cameras set up in the lobby, but when doors and windows were smashed nothing was done about it. The owners of the building eventually kicked everyone out and sold the land to southern developers to build another high rise. But when it was just Clayton and me, we closed ourselves off from the outside world. As long as I was with Clayton, I felt like I was home. We played house until our short-lived peace came to a crashing halt when I found out I was pregnant.

I knew something was off when I threw up from the smell of Clayton's cooking. I hadn't been keeping track of my period, so I couldn't tell if I was late, but I went to the drug store and bought a cheap test just in case. I peed on the stick in the closest public restroom I could find. Sure enough, it was positive.

"You're just gonna have to take care of it," said Clayton when I told him.

I was shocked. "Like, keep it?"

"No. An abortion," he said.

We were on the same page. I didn't want to have a baby. Not now. Not ever. I feared that having a child would turn me into my mother.

During the surgery, I woke up. Even back then, doctors had stopped calling it an abortion. Instead they referred to it as a "procedure" to make it sound less controversial. I just wanted it over and done with, but I woke up as the doctor was using the suction hose. My eyes were open but I couldn't move. I looked up and saw a hanging mobile above me, the kind you see in baby cribs. Why of all things would they put that there? My heart rate started to speed up, but I think my blood pressure must have decreased because I could feel myself slipping away. The machine beside the nurse started beeping frantically and the doctor gave orders to inject me with something to bring my vitals back up. I drifted back into nothingness and woke again, this time to a barren and hollow version of myself.

I still felt pregnant long after the abortion. Was there such a thing as a phantom pregnancy? I stress-ate a lot and began to gain weight rapidly.

Clayton didn't say it outright, but I could sense he was losing his attraction to me. He opted to sleep on the couch most nights. Which is why I found it odd that he would buy me chocolates for my birthday.

"Tastes like rum. Yum!" He laughed as he popped one of the bite-sized chocolates in his mouth, proud of his simple rhyming skills.

As I admired the flowers and teddy bear he had bought me to go along with the box of chocolates, he asked, "What's in those things anyway?"

"I don't know, you're the one who bought them."

"Read the instructions," he huffed, and took a big exhale leaving his tongue hanging out.

"Cocao … haze …" I stopped; the next word was too hard. I didn't want Clayton to know I didn't know how to read.

"Hazelnuts?" He tried to swallow but clearly couldn't.

"Yeah, I think. Why, what's wrong?" I leaned into him and put my hand on his back.

"I'm allergic." He gripped his throat.

"Oh my god."

"I'll be fine, just need some allergy pills."

"Maybe we should go to the hospital?"

He shook his head.

"No. Just call a cab."

"Can you step on it please? It's an emergency," I said to the cab driver as we rushed to the pharmacy but the pharmacist took one look at him and said, "Allergy meds ain't gonna do it for you buddy. You better get yourself to the hospital. Do you want me to call an ambulance?"

By then Clayton was sucking in as much air as he could and his face looked like a balloon. When we got to the hospital in a cab because Clayton was too macho to call an ambulance, the nurses wheeled him into one of the back rooms immediately and started administering an IV.

I sat in the corner of the room for hours waiting for Clayton to start looking like himself again. I ended up stress-eating the rest of the chocolates in one sitting when we got home that evening to be rid of them.

～

Hanging my bare legs off the side of the bed one morning, I noticed that one of my legs was the size of two of Clayton's put together.

I lifted my leg up and gravity made my leg look slender from the top when my skin formed around my thigh bone. But when I looked underneath, the fat drooped lifelessly.

I became obsessed with my weight. When I woke, the first thing I did was regret how much I ate the day before. I would make a promise to myself that I wouldn't overindulge again, but would never be able to keep it. Would Clayton still love me if I gained weight? If my looks changed? Or was he shallow? I mean, he had stayed by my side when I developed a rash that I thought was scabies. When the scabies cream didn't work I admitted myself to the emergency room at the hospital — only to be told it was most likely an allergic reaction to the laundry soap we'd been using. Sure enough, the rash disappeared after we switched detergents.

We had laughed about it then. "You even had me thinking I had the bugs," Clayton said. His voice was caring.

For the short time we had been together, Clayton stood by me. He helped me cope with my irrational fears. He even helped me when I was having night terrors. Sometimes in the middle of the night I'd wake, gasping for air, and Clayton was right there beside me, patting my back and offering me water. Before Clayton, I never thought I would know how it felt to be cared for. I didn't even know how to care for myself.

There wasn't much that I didn't like about Clayton. He was good to me. I felt safe with him. He might have had it rough growing up too, but I couldn't be sure because he veered away from talking about his childhood.

"I never want to go back there," he'd say. I didn't blame him. Neither did I.

I tried my best to play the role of what I thought a girlfriend was supposed to be — domesticated. I had heard that the best way to a man's heart was through his stomach. The only problem was I didn't really know how to cook aside from microwaving or boiling noodles. One night I set out to try and impress him by making fried chicken, knowing how much he loved KFC. I turned the burner on the stove to high and poured the oil in the pan.

"Wow. You're cookin'?" he asked when he walked in the door, back from what I could only guess was one of his drug runs. Clayton sold pot on the side; otherwise he wouldn't have been able to afford the things he did on his monthly government cheque.

"Yeah, I thought I'd give it a try."

"Watcha making?" He came up behind me as I was cutting the chicken on the countertop.

I thought for a second I could smell perfume coming off him, but I couldn't be sure.

"Your favourite," I said proudly.

"Oh yeah. How'd you know chicken was my favourite?"

"Oh, come on, you're at KFC every other day," I joked.

"Okay, okay," he laughed, "but can you make it like the Colonel?"

"You'll have to wait and see, I guess," I flirted.

But there would be no dinner because the oil caught fire. I forgot I had it on high.

By the time I spun around, the fire had reached the hood of the stove, though it was still contained within the pan.

"Oh no!" I cried.

Clayton panicked and started running around the kitchen in circles looking for something to put it out with.

"I forgot it was on!" In a mix of embarrassment and failure, I tried to reach around the flames and turn the stove off but burned my arm.

"Water. We need water," Clayton yelled.

"No! Water'll just make it worse." I looked around for something to smother it with.

"Where's the fire extinguisher?" Clayton said frantically as he pulled random items out from under the kitchen sink throwing them over his shoulder.

I grabbed a plate and covered the flames, but the fire raged underneath cracking the ceramic in half.

"We need flour," I said, trying to remain calm as I hit the fire with the dish towel. "The cupboard," I said as I pointed to the cupboard on my left. "No, the other cupboard," I said when he opened the wrong one.

He found the yellow bag of flour and dumped the entire contents onto the stove until it looked like a winter storm had blown into our tiny kitchen, dampening the fire.

"That was close!" he said and leaned back on the counter, sweat dripping down his face. He laughed. "That was real close," he said again and put his hand on his chest to feel how fast his heart was beating.

"I'm sorry," I said. Deep down I was kicking myself. Another fire, Nyla? Seriously?

"Since when do we have flour?" Clayton asked. Maybe he was trying to change the subject to make me feel better.

"The food bank." A grocery bag full of non-perishables was placed outside the apartment door every other week whether we needed it or not, and the cupboards were full of loads of the same three ingredients: powdered milk, sugar and flour.

There were still bits of crumbs on fire under the burner and Clayton took pleasure in hitting them with the dish towel.

"Let's stick to KFC from now on," he said and hugged me close. I put my head on his chest and felt like crying. Seeing how upset I was, he continued. "Hey, don't take it so hard. At least you didn't burn the place down."

Later, as I struggled to scrub the burned clumps of flour off the inside of the pan, I couldn't help but think that all I was good at was causing destruction.

I gave up and threw the whole pan out with the blackened dishcloth. Black ashes streaked across my forehead as I wiped my brow. I was a marked woman, haunted by a past that didn't seem to want to let me go.

When I found out Clayton had been cheating on me, I didn't want to believe it. But looking back, he had started to become more guarded about his whereabouts. Almost defensive. He would stay out later and later. He didn't come home at all some nights. His drinking was getting out of control — or maybe it always was but only then had I really noticed. He no longer seemed present even when he was around. One night he came home so drunk he swayed in the middle of the apartment in the dark.

"Deidra," he called out when he saw me lying on the couch watching TV.

"My name's not Deidra. What the hell, Clayton? Are you serious right now?"

He came over to me and tried to lie down beside me, but I was too upset and stormed to the other side of the room where the bed was. Who was Deidra? Did he love her? I knew things had changed between us since the pregnancy, but this was too much to take.

I watched him grab a beer from the fridge and crack it open before he chugged it and crushed the can loudly in his fist. Then he walked to the bathroom and shut the door. He was back and forth from the fridge to the bathroom until I couldn't take it anymore. What was he up to?

I walked slowly and quietly towards the bathroom door, put my ear up to it and listened but couldn't hear a sound. I opened the door slowly, just enough to peek inside. He was sitting on the toilet seat, bent over the tub.

The white lines running across the side of the tub made my heart drop. He was in the middle of cutting a line with his bank card when I stepped inside.

"What are you doing?"

"Come on, Nyla."

"I thought you were done with that shit!" I cried.

He stood up and plowed past me, grabbing his jacket.

"You want to go back out? Fine. Get out," I said and pushed him to the front door. He didn't argue. He wanted a reason to leave.

I didn't see him until a few days later when he came to get some of his stuff. I was just getting out of the shower and had my towel wrapped around me. There was a big gap on the side from where the cloth landed on my hip. I had to hold it together when I bent over, or it would bust open with the weight I gained.

"You're leaving? Just like that? Leaving me alone in your apartment? What about all your stuff?"

"Keep it." His tone was short and uncaring. I threw all my questions at him, but he dodged every one of them.

"Is it 'cause I gained weight? I'm not good enough for you anymore, is that it? You used me, Clayton. You used me just like everyone else! That's not love." I got louder and angrier with each accusation, each one a revelation I didn't want to accept as truth.

Even though he stayed silent, I could see that he was getting heated. His face had turned red. He was holding back.

"Just say it, Clayton. Just say it. You don't love me anymore. You never really loved me. If you did you wouldn't leave me like this."

"Nyla, just stop already. I'm done. Move on. I'm moving on. Why can't you? You're acting crazy."

I couldn't take it anymore. I attacked him with every ounce of strength I had in me. I scratched his face up with my nails like a wild animal until he bled.

He grabbed me by the wrists and pinned me down on the couch and my towel flew open. "Enough, Nyla. It's over."

"I hate you! I hate you!" I yelled and struggled to get out of his grip but he was too strong so I spit on him. He reacted by punching me hard on the cheek. I was so shocked that he hit me that I stopped crying and held my face, looking at him wide-eyed. He let me go and stood over me as I lay there frozen in heartbreak.

"I'm sorry," he said and tried to help me up.

"No! I don't need you," I lied. I needed him. I wanted him. Wanted him to hold me and never leave me.

He looked at my naked body and I felt ashamed and covered myself with my towel. "You've changed, Nyla. I don't even recognize you anymore."

If I'd known then what I know now, I wouldn't have wanted to be with someone like him. I thought he had more depth. But since I had no self-worth, I believed him.

He grabbed the things he came there for and walked to the door. I wanted to run and try to stop him from leaving but it would be no use. His mind was made up.

Before leaving, he turned around. "I promised I'd never hit a woman. When I was a kid, all I saw was my dad hittin' my mom, and I swore I'd never lay a hand on a woman but you made me do it, Nyla. You made me." His lips were trembling. I hung on to his every word. Maybe I did deserve it.

After he left, I stopped eating, stopped sleeping. I could very well have stopped breathing. Even when I was utterly exhausted, I couldn't bring myself to close my eyes. I slept in his imprint, where the mattress formed to his body. My agoraphobia came back full force.

With Clayton gone, I wasn't sure how I was going to survive. Even though I had everything I needed, I was still barely able to function on my own. I didn't need to pay rent, I had a roof over my head, I had food brought to me each week, even though I didn't eat it and lost weight drastically in a short amount of time. At the end of the day I was still alone and heartbroken and didn't know what to do with myself. Like the belongings Clayton left behind, I had become a temporary fixture too, nothing more than a piece of old dusty furniture to him.

To try and drown my sorrows I ran the water the hottest it could go in the shower and leaned against the stained yellow tile, but it wasn't enough. I got to my knees and curled into a ball, scalding my back but nothing could take away the thought of him.

I needed closure. I needed to talk to him one more time.

I forced myself to leave the apartment. Maybe I let him walk away too easily. Maybe I had to fight for him.

I went to the usual spots he hung out at and found out where he was staying. People like to gossip in small towns and soon enough I found out Clayton was already shacked up.

I don't remember how I got there, but I found myself standing outside the apartment where he had his new life. A colourful, two-story townhome down the hill from the rocks where I met Alex, which seemed like a lifetime ago. I walked up to the door and listened. I could hear the TV blaring. Then footsteps.

Then a voice.

"Just going to the store, babe. Want anything?" Her voice became clearer the closer she got to the door.

"Grab me a few more, will ya?" The man's voice was muffled. It could have been anyone, but when I heard a can crack open followed by a crushing sound, I knew it was Clayton.

The doorknob turned and I quickly hid behind the stairs leading up to the unit above as she walked out to her car. I could see through the entrance window that she was pretty. She had long, black hair and thick, straight bangs. Her overbite showed off her bright, white teeth. Her skin was dark against her yellow shirt. Worst of all, she was tall and slim like a supermodel.

After she left, without a second thought I brazenly opened the unlocked door to the unit and let myself in. I walked straight into the living room where Clayton sat, exposing my ugly bruise to him.

"Look what you did to me," I said opening my mouth to show him the dark blue bruise on the inside of my cheek where he punched me. It would take over a month to subside. It wasn't the first thing I planned to say to him but it was the first thing that came to mind as my heart raced.

"Holy shit, Nyla. What the hell are you doing here?" He jumped off the couch in fright and looked past me to see if his new girlfriend was close by.

"So, she's what you left me for?" I pointed back at the door.

"How'd you get in here? Get out before I call the cops. You're crazy."

"Crazy! Really, Clayton? Crazy? That's all you have to say?" I cried, seething in his betrayal.

He walked towards me fast and pushed me backwards out the door, slamming it in my face and locking it behind me. "Get out and don't come back," he said with a huff. I should have left then, but I sat at the top of the stairs inside the complex, waiting for her to get back home to tell her to leave him alone. It was all I could do.

Who was I without Clayton? We were soulmates — he'd said so. "Twin flames" were his exact words.

When I heard the keys turning in the door to the common area, I changed my mind about confronting her and hid behind the wall at the top of the stairs. Did she even know he left me for her? Would she even care to know what that felt like? She turned the knob to walk into her apartment only to realize it was locked. She knocked and spoke softly through the door.

"Clayton? Why'd you lock it?" She got her keys back out and shuffled around for the right one, but he opened the door before she could get to it.

I ducked, knowing he'd be looking over her shoulder for any sign of me. Maybe he was afraid I would hurt her. I heard the door lock followed by their whispered voices. He was telling her about me.

Maybe if I fixed myself up. If I lost more weight. If I got a haircut and better clothes. If I looked like her. Maybe he would come back to me.

I never wanted to go back to the life I once lived on the street or crashing at Carli's house, but I convinced myself that I needed the money if I wanted to get him back.

I went back to the man who ran the corner store across from the busy bar where most of the homeless panhandled for change. He was a family man. He served banana splits and vanilla sundaes with extra sprinkles on top to kids. His wife worked the lottery booth and cashed in scratch tickets, and his kids stocked the shelves every day after school. I walked in during the day when I knew he'd be working alone. His wife did their banking around the same time each week. I knew her routine just by hanging around outside. She was quiet and observant, which made me think she knew all about his double life. He, on the other hand, was extra friendly with the customers. Always laughing and joking.

I walked in, gave him a fake smile as I pretended to scour the different flavoured bags of chips.

When the only customer left, I walked up to the till. "I need to borrow a few bucks."

He nodded. "Seven o'clock," was all he needed to say.

It was still light out when I got to his empty apartment. The only thing in it was a bed in the middle of the living room floor with a few sheets tacked up over the window to hide his sins from the world. He ushered me in and quickly shut the door behind me. He wanted to get it over with fast. Did he know I was underage? He had to have known back then when I was much younger.

He lay down on the bed after stripping naked, without shame. Before joining him I boldly demanded, "I want the money first this time. All of it, not that half-now-half-later bullshit."

He looked over at the white envelope on the upside-down cardboard box meant to serve as an end table. He had no reason to think this time would be any different. No reason to think he was about to be ripped off. I grabbed the envelope, looked inside, and tucked it into the back pocket of my jeans.

I took my shirt off and started to remove my ratty push-up bra but stopped. "I've gotta use the washroom first."

He pointed to the hallway to the left, like I didn't know where to find the washroom, like I hadn't been there before.

Inside, I stared at myself in the mirror trying to build up the courage to run out the door.

"Never again," I whispered to myself. Even though I hadn't much in the way of self-worth, it was enough.

I tiptoed out of the bathroom to the front door, hoping he wouldn't see me but he did. "Hey, where you going?"

With my shirt in one hand and the envelope now shoved under my arm, I ran to the door and fumbled with the small chain lock. It took forever to slide open, but when it did, I bolted into the hallway and headed for the stairs. He stood in the doorway with a blanket across his waist, shaking his fist at me in silence before giving up and going back inside.

The first thing I did was buy a new outfit. Then I got bangs, but the hairdresser wasn't very good — she even nicked my ear — and my hair ended up looking more like a mullet. Nowhere near Deidra's.

The money didn't get me very far. It never did. The last of it was spent on a bottle that I bought off a taxi driver selling booze out of his trunk.

As inebriated as I was, I somehow found my way back to the door that separated me from Clayton's new life. It was the middle of the night when I got down on my knees, not to pray, but to slip a small piece of paper under his door, a love letter. In it, I wanted to pour my heart out, pleading for him to change his mind and come back to me, but I didn't have the words so I left it blank.

As a symbol of the love within that still burned for him, I twisted and lit the paper on fire before sliding it under the small gap between the heavy steel door and the grey carpeted flooring of his unit. I was only going to let it burn for a second and pull it back through, leaving nothing but the ashes of our love for him to find the next morning, but I pushed the paper too far and couldn't retrieve it. I waited a few moments, listening at the door. I don't know what I expected to hear, I just hoped it would die out. But the steel door soon became too hot against my ear. I'd caught the carpet on fire.

I had to warn him, but the sound of the smoke alarm beat me to it.

I can only remember flashes of what happened after that. I remember worrying about the children that might be trapped inside. I cared, I know I did, I felt it. I think I tried kicking down the door but it was of no use.

I know at some point I gave up and ran away before the fire trucks arrived. I stopped at the park across the street and stood next to a tire swing swaying in the wind. I saw the doors of the townhomes fly open and one by one people ran out with their jackets halfway on, hopping on one foot trying to get into their shoes as their homes burned behind them.

Clayton and his new lover were nowhere to be seen. Would they be able to get out through the front door before it was too late? Or would they have to jump off the balcony at the back of the building? Even though they were on the ground floor, the windows of their unit were high up. The complex was built on stilts because of the marshland the building backed onto. There was no way the fire trucks could get to the back of the building through the swampy waters of the shallow pond. It was full of muskrats and wasn't deep enough to safely jump into from above.

The familiar sound of fire trucks, paired with my thundering heartbeat, roared closer and closer. I could hear heavy sirens racing towards the fire that had by then engulfed the front of the building, where large flames billowed through the roof like dark clouds.

Not able to face the damage I'd done, I weaved in and around endless apartment buildings and rowhomes in a big half circle until I reached the cliffs that overlooked the muskrat pond, hoping for any sight of him. I stayed there until it was over. Until I was sober.

The next morning, I crawled out from under the rocks and walked back down the hill to witness the devastation. Fire trucks were still outside on standby; black smoke continued to pollute the fresh morning air. The entire row of units was burned right down to the frame. I walked past the fire trucks, trying not to stare at the destruction I created, thinking that if they made eye contact with me they'd see the guilt. I kept walking, through the field next to the park where I had stood helplessly the night before. This time it was filled with kids laughing and playing innocently. Some of them pointed at the burned rowhome with eyes wide. I must have looked like a monster, the way they looked at me in fear. I felt like one.

I looked back one last time at the wreckage before heading back to the transition house. Did Clayton survive? If he were still alive, would he know I did this? I wasn't afraid of being caught this time. I deserved to be behind bars.

Maybe they'd come looking for me if the police asked Clayton if he had any enemies. Would they be able to tell if the building was set fire on purpose or would they know it was an accident? I would confess to everything. Clayton didn't know about my affinity with fire. The urge had subsided when he was around.

I wanted to reach out to him. To find out if he was okay. I needed to know he was still alive. To my surprise, he beat me to it when he called me from the hospital in utter angst. I knew it had to be him when I heard the phone ring. No one else ever called. As much as I wished he was calling to tell me what I'd been longing to hear, that he loved me and wanted me back, I knew that wasn't the reason why he was calling.

His voice was cold. "I know it was you," he said shakily. It was clear he was having difficulty breathing.

"I didn't mean it!" I blurted.

"I'm in the fucking hospital right now with my leg in a splint, Nyla. You're lucky no one died!" He yelled with what energy he had left in him. "I had to jump out the fucking window!"

I wanted to ask him if it was worse than the time he jumped out of a third-story balcony after a break-and-enter he did that went wrong, but this was far beyond that so I just offered up a weak apology. "I'm sorry. It was an accident."

"Jesus. There were kids in there sleeping."

I knew this. I had the TV constantly turned on since he left to drown out the noise of my own thoughts. The one free channel I had played TV bingo every evening followed by a listing of events around town and then the local news. I watched one of the victims in tears, devastated by the loss of everything she owned. "My photographs, my keepsakes, everything is gone," she said in despair. "I hope they find who did this."

Arson was already suspected. A thousand apologies would never be enough.

"You're going away, Nyla. You're going away for a long time."

"It was an accident!" I cried.

"Why'd you do it, Nyla. Why?"

"I wanted you to leave her. I don't know. I wasn't thinking," I said truthfully.

"Stay the hell away from me. I mean it," he said and hung up.

I thought about running, but I couldn't move. My skin felt like it was on fire.

Then, I heard a knock at the door.

That day I learned the police have a very specific kind of knock. There's an urgency in it. Would they kick the door down if I didn't answer?

I got dressed slowly and took my time before opening the door to four officers with guns pointed. If they'd ended my life right then and there, I wouldn't have cared.

I held my trembling hands out and surrendered.

SIX

It'd been years since I'd seen Em but there she was, the same as ever, sitting behind me as I stood next to the young inexperienced lawyer representing me in the courtroom. Was she there for me?

I looked down and fidgeted with my hands as the judge read my sentence. The prosecutor had asked for attempted murder plus arson, but because I pled guilty I was only charged with arson; I could have walked away if I pled not guilty. They had no real evidence, only a private confession to an ex-boyfriend. There were no witnesses. It had been dark. It could have been anyone.

At the time, I thought it best that I be locked away forever. I couldn't be in the world without leaving a trail of devastation behind me wherever I went. Fire had become my weapon of destruction.

Turns out Em wasn't there for me; she just happened to be in the courtroom that morning because it was her job. She was a volunteer at a community justice non-profit organization; she was taking a gap year after graduating from high school. My lawyer suggested I participate in a community program to lessen my sentence, and I initially agreed. But during the break when he brought me into a little office outside of the court room to meet with Em and discuss my options for diversion, I changed my mind.

"I guess your dad was right all along about me, hey?" I said facetiously.

"I'm here to help you, Nyla."

"Why?"

"It's my job."

"So let me get this straight, you're not here to see me. You're here because it's your job?"

"Both?" she asked rhetorically. "When I saw your name on the court docket, I wanted to come see you and asked to help with your possible diversion process."

"Well, I'm a high-profile criminal now, so you probably can't help me anyway," I said flatly.

"Nyla." The way she said my name sounded sympathetic. "You had a tough upbringing. I know you have a good heart. You're not a bad person."

It was time she knew. "Remember Noah?"

"Of course, I remember Noah."

"I did it."

"Did what?"

"I started the fire," I said, staring at her without blinking.

"It was an accident." Her once-certain words now sounded more like a question. She became visibly upset as she put all the scattered pieces together of my lifelong compulsion to fire. "It *was* an accident, right?"

I put my head down. "I don't know anymore."

She stiffened and then remembered she had to act professionally. "You can't change the past, Nyla, but you might have an opportunity to get help. Is that something you think you might want?" She was taking notes now.

Who could help someone like me? I wanted to ask but I just sat there looking at the floor contemplating my options.

"Listen. I know it's not the best time to tell you, but I don't know when else I'll have a chance. Your mom came to my dad's apartment looking for you. She wanted you to know she's not well. She's really ..." She was searching for the right word to say as I slowly took my eyes off the floor. "Weak," she said finally, her voice soft.

"Weak?" I asked. I never knew the woman to be weak.

"Yes. She has liver disease. Your aunt has been taking care of her."

"Things couldn't get any worse I guess, right?" I said, trying not to care.

And in a way, I didn't. Not at that moment, anyway. It worried me. How could I not feel any sadness and concern over the woman who gave me life — even if it was a life I didn't want? It was just as well, I told myself; she was never a mother to me anyway.

"I'm not doing community work. Lock me up." I got up quickly and turned my back to Em as I waited for the lawyer to open the door.

"Nyla." Em reached out her hand.

I ignored her and the lawyer brought me back into the custody of the guard, who led me back into the court cells to await my sentence.

Jail wasn't as bad as they made it out to be on TV. Not compared to the streets or Carli's house or even my mother's house for that matter. I battled boredom by trying to learn to sew like the other inmates but didn't have the patience for it. I did finally learn how to cook though. Jail was structured, disciplined and always cold. Everything was steel grey. Steel bars, steel beds, steel guards.

The hardest part was when the lights went out for the night. The guards made sure we didn't have anything in our cells that we could hurt ourselves with.

No matter what, I could never get used to using the toilet in front of the girl I shared a cell with. That and the smell of orange cleaning solution. Any citrus-scented products now and forever will remind me of my time behind bars.

My cellmate's name was Charmaine. She was serving time for attacking her boyfriend while she was black-out drunk. She looked so familiar to me, I could have sworn she'd attacked me once when I was in the bathroom of a bar. She had walked in completely obliterated, and a girl doing her makeup in the mirror beside me as I washed my hands laughed at her. Charmaine, or someone who looked exactly like her, attacked me when I walked out, thinking that I had been the one laughing at her. I managed to get away from her but she was vicious, pulling out a chunk of my hair as the crowd around us watched and cheered. The bouncer broke up the fight and threw her out of the bar kicking and screaming while I went back into the washroom to try to fix myself up. It wasn't my first time taking a punch.

Charmaine didn't seem to remember me, and I would have been foolish to remind her.

"What you in for?"

"I burned down a building."

"Holy shit, girl, that's crazy," she said, like it was a contest.

"Why are you here?" I was afraid to know the answer.

"Me? My old man used to rough me up and … everything happened so fast."

Accidents are like that, I said to myself.

"I protected myself, that's all. How did I know he was gonna die?" She looked at me as if I had the answer to the question she would ask herself for the rest of her life.

Charmaine rubbed both her temples vigorously as a tear fell from her expressionless eyes.

Then she smiled. "He was always joking around, getting along with everyone. That's how I'm gonna remember him."

The cafeteria was the only place we could go outside of our cell aside from the yard. I could go outside if I wanted to and walk around in circles, fenced in, but it made me feel like a wild animal. Besides, it was too cold most days with the jail being right on the lake. Thankfully, I didn't care to be outside all that much. My agoraphobia was still intense, but I was just glad I didn't have a problem with claustrophobia, having to be confined to a small room for the remainder of my sentence.

It was a small jail that could only house a handful of women at a time. Most of the inmates came from the more remote communities. Many of them had been lost in the broken system from a young age, often abused like Charmaine, and then punished for finally defending themselves. Most everyone played cards to pass the time. Some were carvers, carving elaborate animals out of soapstone and crosses out of wood to give away as gifts.

I just sat there most days, watching mind-numbing TV until summer rolled around and the guards suggested we form a softball team to play against them for fun. Charmaine bullied her way into being team captain and started bossing everyone around, telling them what position they'd play. She was a good leader that way, I guess. She must have known I was a horrible athlete because she put me on as back catcher. I didn't want to play but didn't really feel like I had a choice. We didn't have time to practise, either.

The first team up to bat was decided with a coin toss. A lot of the other girls struck out every time they were at bat, but I was a sure thing. I hit the ball every time. I only hit grounders. Lucky for us they worked because the pitcher couldn't catch a grounder if he tried with his big beer belly in the way.

Grounders made my mediocre skills as a back catcher forgivable. I felt like I was good at something for once. When I fluked out and caught a foul, everyone cheered but I didn't know why until the guard told me I got him automatically out just by catching it.

If only life were that easy. I never really did learn the rules of the game, which would have been helpful. When one of the guards came running to home base and the ball was flying in my direction, I wasn't sure what to do with it once I caught it in my ill-fitted glove. I looked to Charmaine for answers.

"Tag him. Tag him!" Charmaine yelled from the bench. I tried tagging him but we collided and I felt like I hit a brick wall. I was lucky that all I suffered was a sprained toe.

Even with a sprained toe my best skill was running. I could have outrun anyone in the field and always made it to first base, thanks to my grounders. The guards soon nicknamed me "Wind in Her Hair," — which, I won't lie, I kind of liked.

Just when I started to get more confident, my shining glory

ended as quickly as it had started. The guards figured out my predictable play and made it their mission to get me out. The pitcher finally caught one of my grounders and whipped the ball so hard to first base just as I was rounding the base that the ball hit me right in the back of the head when the first baseman missed the pass. I didn't fall down. I just crouched and held my head with both hands. My team rushed over to see if I was okay. Charmaine walked me back to the bench slowly while one of the guards went to the kitchen to get me some ice.

"Home run. Home run. Home run," my team chanted.

I must have looked confused because the warden gave a nod and said, "Go on."

I took my ice with me and walked the diamond from base to base until I made it home. My first and only home run.

After that I wasn't able to run to first base anymore without stopping short of the mat and checking to see if a ball was flying in my direction. "Just put on a helmet," Charmaine said and everyone laughed. "I'm good. I'll just sit one out." I wasn't about to be the only one wearing one. I didn't care that much about winning. Charmaine did though, and my team needed me because they ended up losing pretty badly to the guards in the final game of the season. With all we'd been through, they should have just let us win.

Something about the perimeter of the yard around me made me feel safe.

I made an honest effort to learn how to read. I made my bed. I took care of my hygiene. Who would have known that in jail I would learn how to properly use utensils? Strangely, jail was structured in a way that there was consistency in it. I felt good about doing the dishes after dinner. Small things were part of life. A normal life. Doing those things made me feel closer to normal than I ever had before, and I craved it.

But as they say, old habits die hard, and I was still impressionable.

"Hey. You know they keep the keys in the skidoos," Charmaine said quietly as she walked into our shared cell. I was comfortably lying down on the bottom bunk watching a talk show on the small TV we shared. The cell doors were kept open during the day, for us to come and go freely throughout the building as long as we were on good behaviour.

"Oh. And?"

"That's our ticket."

"Our?"

"I can't take it anymore. I don't wanna be stuck in here another four years. I'd rather be dead." It was clear that Charmaine was having another one of her bad days.

"What happened this time?"

"Just sick of those damn guards telling me what to do all the time." She raised her voice to make sure they could hear her. One of them walked by, looking at her as if to say, one wrong move and she'd be put in isolation again.

"How long you got left in here anyway? You just going to keep sitting here like that day after day?"

At that point I didn't know how much more time I had left. I had stopped counting. Where was I going to go when I got out anyway? Jail was home now. As sad as that was to contemplate.

"I can't do it alone," Charmaine stood in front of the TV so that I had no choice but to pay full attention to her.

"What? Escape?"

"Shhh. Don't say it so loud."

"And where exactly would we go?" I lowered my voice but still sounded skeptical. I was far from sold on the idea.

"Anywhere but here."

I thought about it for a minute then said, "I'll help you, but I'm not going with you."

My part in Charmaine's plan was to create a diversion. I'd distract the guards so she could climb the fence to the skidoos. It almost seemed too easy. She'd ride away into the sunset as she made her way across the lake and to freedom. The only problem was, there were two skidoos.

"I need you to take one. Even if you're not coming with me, I just need you to drive it around the back and hide it so they can't get on it and follow me."

"They're gonna think I'm trying to escape too."

"No, they won't even see you. I'll get you back I promise."

I hoped I'd never need her help, ever. I wish I had thought then to tell her to throw the other skidoo key in the snowbank, but it didn't cross my mind until it was too late.

I didn't know when she was planning on escaping. I just waited for Charmaine to say the magic words.

Then one day, out of the blue, she said it, "Bugs and drugs." It was our inside joke about what she'd be going back to once she made her escape, to living in her rundown housing unit.

She started walking towards the door that led out to the shared common area outside. I followed after a while. The guards were all in the main living area just off the cafeteria, watching TV with the inmates. It looked more like a hospice rather than a correctional facility. There were so few of us locked up, the guards were never on high alert.

"Now what? I asked as I shivered in the cold.

Charmaine had her jacket stowed away in a bush behind the smoking area and threw it on.

"Where's your jacket?"

"Thanks, mom. I'm not going with you, remember," I said sarcastically.

"Your loss."

I'm not the one who's about to get caught, I said to myself.

"This is goodbye, I guess. It was nice getting to know ya, jailmate," she said, smiling from ear to ear as if she were already free.

Charmaine made jumping the wire fence look easy. There was a thin, flimsy layer of barbed wire at the top that she got snagged up on for only a second.

"Come on," she said in a hurried hush as she bent low.

I started climbing while looking back through the side window at the guards to see if they had caught on yet, thankful to see the back of their heads.

I got hung up at the top of the fence and nearly fell over onto the other side, but Charmaine grabbed my foot and helped lower me down.

"We gotta start 'em at the same time," she said and jumped on the blue skidoo facing the lake, leaving me with the red one beside it.

"They're easy starters, no need to pull on the rope. Just turn the key and rev it on my count."

At the count of three mine wouldn't start. Hers on the other hand started like a gem and sat there sputtering loudly. I used to love the smell of gas fumes lingering in the brisk air, but there was no time to relish it. I looked towards the window again thinking surely the guards would have caught onto us by then, but the windows were soundproof and they couldn't hear the noisy engine idling.

"Hurry up, Nyla."

"I don't know how."

Charmaine jumped off her skidoo and ran over to me.

"Take mine," she said and pushed me off.

She jumped on the red skidoo and started it with ease.

"Let's go."

"But …" I didn't know how to turn the big machine around to hide it around the corner like we had planned. Then I heard one of the guards yell, "Hey!"

Charmaine flew past the window in the peripheral vision of the guards who all got up and bolted towards the scene. They saw my face as clear as day. Afraid of the consequences of getting caught, I reluctantly followed Charmaine straight out into the middle of the lake.

We cut a trail more than halfway across the long, narrow lake until the skidoos slowed to a stop. We had run out of gas.

"Now what?" I asked in a panic.

"I don't know. Let me think." She tapped her forehead with her fist. I was shaking in my thin green jail pants and matching shirt. Charmaine wouldn't have noticed that I was freezing to death had I not asked her if she had an extra jacket inside the pillowcase she used to stuff her belongings. All she had was an extra pair of slippers her grandmother had given her and a knitted sweater. It was better than nothing.

"They'll be coming for us soon," she said as she tried to light a cigarette, but the relentless wind coming off the lake kept blowing out the flame.

"We need to get into the trees." I at least knew that much, as much as I wanted to be found at that point. I knew we had to make a fire immediately or both of us would freeze to death.

My ankles were burning in pain from wearing slippers and socks in the snow. As we trudged our way towards the trees, I thought I heard the skidoos but it was a helicopter fast approaching until it was close enough to hover directly above us. I waved my arms in the air in surrender, but when Charmaine made it to the tree line and disappeared, I had to make a decision fast.

The small voice inside said go back, but when I heard Charmaine yelling "Nyla, c'mon, hurry up!" I ran in her direction.

I couldn't trust myself to make the right decision, but I could trust myself to make a fire.

Outside our shared cell, Charmaine was an entirely different person. She was a known bully around town. She was bigger than most girls, not only in the physical sense but in the way she carried herself.

"She was larger than life," her family would all say after she died. People often say that after people die, but it was true about Charmaine. She was rowdy and full of drama. If you met her, you'd never forget her. We would have never been friends, if you could call us that, if we hadn't met in jail. Charmaine was the type of person that would put you down in a joking kind of way so that you would have to laugh at yourself in front of the crowd even if you didn't find the joke funny. She was a sniper, always armed and ready to pick on some unassuming innocent victim.

After our escape, Charmaine and I found our way back to Coppertown and crashed with her friends who were willing to harbour a couple of fugitives, but we didn't hide out long even though our faces were plastered in the local news. We cut our hair and bleached it blonde, thinking we would somehow be unrecognizable, but our hair turned orange making us that much more noticeable.

The long nights of partying and passing out with random strangers got old fast. How did I find my way back here again? I was no longer worried about getting caught. At least I'd have a place to rest my head every night and a guaranteed meal instead of wondering where I'd end up from day to day.

Charmaine's friends could always be found day drinking on a set of stairs leading up to a used furniture store off Coppertown's main drag. There was always some sort of fight going on, but when two of them started squabbling over the last sip out of the bottle, the only blonde, blue-eyed girl out of all of us was clunked on the head with it. I couldn't just stand there and watch her get beat up, so I tried to help her and the stairs suddenly turned into a boxing ring.

When the cops came to break it up, I was at another crossroad. This time I didn't run.

Charmaine got away but years later I found out she died in a car accident, speeding down the highway, drinking and driving with those same friends. They hit a power pole head on. No one survived.

SEVEN

A homeless musician I used to hang out with on occasion once broke into someone's house and stabbed a dog. As horrible of a person as I was, I was thankful that I wasn't a dog killer. I can't say I entirely blame him for what he did though. He needed shelter from the cold night and was off his meds. Being in and out of jail most of his life, he knew what it would take to get himself back behind bars. I didn't, but still found myself back there anyway.

I was on maximum-security lockdown for half a year, and they added more time to my sentence after the jail break. It was enough to satisfy the judge that I would learn my lesson and be rehabilitated. When they felt sure I was no longer a flight risk, they again presented me with the option of diversion so I could leave jail before I finished my sentence. When I asked about Em and if she was still volunteering, they told me she decided to go off to college to be a social worker. I never pegged Em as the type to be a social worker; I figured she'd go into fashion.

I was the only one left in the jail when it was time for my release. It had been a small group of us to begin with. Those who committed petty crimes like theft spent some time in jail but were diverted into their home community where they did sentencing circles.

The number of guards watching over me was laughable. The facility was paying full-time wages to government employees who worked minimal hours twiddling their thumbs to guard one prisoner. At night I was left alone in the large, empty building, with the exception of one guard, who played solitaire on his computer and picked his nose when he thought no one was looking.

Near the end of my sentence, the warden felt I was ready to be released into the community to serve the rest of my time, released early on good behaviour they called it. Reintegration was another big word they used, basically to say I would be sent back to my home community. But I didn't know what community I belonged to, so they sent me to a small reserve a few kilometres from the jail. A place that needed "a few extra hands." Supervised by the Chief, I would spend next year of my life living in a teepee for the summer and a camper in the winter months.

When I stepped out of the white corrections van and onto the gravel road outside of the small band office, I was greeted by the Chief. To my surprise, she was a woman.

"You must be Nyla. My name's Cayenne. Glad to see you're coming to spend some time helping out in our community."

"Thanks." Her name wouldn't be hard for me to remember. I had grown to appreciate the use of spices while in jail learning to cook.

"We're having our annual leadership meeting this weekend and we have visitors from all over the North here to elect the new Chief. So, we'll need you to be one of our Firekeepers for the next few days. Are you okay with that?"

"Firekeeper?" I asked, thinking it was a joke. Did they not know my history? I should have been the last person on earth for the job.

"Yes. Firekeepers are tasked with a very special responsibility. You'll be staying in here." She opened the flap of the off-white canvas teepee to show me inside. "You'll have everything you need. The youth will be bringing you wood throughout the night to keep the fire going. Normally women aren't allowed to take on this role but times are changing."

There was a mustard-coloured foam mattress on the ground with a few sleeping blankets rolled into a ball on the end and two pillows in an airtight, clear garbage bag. Above me was a row of logs tied together, forming a shelf for storage.

In the middle of the teepee was a crackling fire.

"We're putting you on nights. You'll be sharing the tent with Calvin, the day shift."

She wasn't kidding — this actually was a legitimate job.

I put my stuff down next to the mattress. It reminded me of the time I ripped a small piece off a foam mattress my mom had in the living room and shoved it up my nose. It got stuck and stayed there for days, weeks, months until my mom started noticing that I smelled bad. Finally, she couldn't take it anymore and took me to the doctor. I think it had to be the first time I'd ever been to the doctor, other than when I was born and the time I needed stitches.

He had looked in my throat, eyes and ears then my nose with a tiny pen light. "Ah, children, they just love shoving things up their nose. This must've been in there for a long time."

"Oh?" my mom said, and the doctor looked at her in surprise as if she should have known. Her neglect was showing. He took a long pair of tweezers and plucked out the rotten fibers that felt like they tickled my brain.

"Do I start now?" I asked Cayenne.

She laughed and said kindly, "You can start this evening. I'll show you where we keep the food in the band office. You should get some rest though. You're gonna need it; you're on the graveyard shift."

I followed her into the band office where a few Elders sat drinking tea while little kids ran around in the middle of the open room.

"Help yourself to anything here. There's lots of food to go around."

I took a few grape juice boxes, filled my pockets with individually wrapped cookies and went back to the empty teepee. A tiny grey mouse scurried out from under the mattress as I sat down, and I threw a cookie crumb at it.

I unrolled one of the sleeping bags and lay down on top of it, watching the single streak of smoke twirl up and out through the small hole at the top of the canvas into the blue sky. I took Cayenne's advice and tried to get some rest before having to stay up all night tending to the fire and lay down and closed my eyes.

I could hear the innocent sounds of children playing and laughing outside the tent. Their happiness began to sound farther and farther away as my thoughts slowly drifted up and out into the sky like the smoke. I sunk further and further down into the foam, my body becoming one with the earth.

I woke to the sound of a loud bang followed by popping noises and people shouting. I quickly shot up and looked to the fire to make sure I hadn't let it go out of control. It burned and crackled steadily inside the confines of the circle of rocks, and relief washed over me.

Then I heard something whistle as it zipped past the tent and another scream came from the crowd outside, filling me with anxiety.

I walked out of the teepee to see what was happening, and there was a crowd standing around watching two older men light fireworks. One had a lit cigarette hanging out of his mouth and the other was attempting to light up what looked to be a roll of dynamite in the middle of the gravel road across from the band office.

"Look out!" Someone shouted as one of the fireworks flew vertically, heading straight for the crowd at eye level. That didn't stop the two men from further lighting up the night sky with random misfired fireworks that fizzled out at the tree line.

I watched for a bit. I'd always wanted to see fireworks, but in the back of my mind I thought about the fire and my duty that awaited. I retreated back to the tent well before they ran out of explosives and started my shift. I sat up all night, putting logs into the fire whenever it got low, careful not to add too much.

I jumped at the sound of a voice in the early hours of the morning as I tried my hardest to stay awake. "It's custom," the other Firekeeper said as he walked in for his shift. "We keep it going to make sure the discussions are guided by our Ancestors. So, whatever you do, don't let it go out." He shuffled the coals around with the fire poker.

"I'm trying."

～

I woke in the early evening to the sound of a dirt bike doing a wheelie next to the teepee. Calvin sat cross-legged on his foamy on the other side of the fire, staring into it intently. He looked across at me.

"Good, you're awake."

He must have heard me stir. Was he there the whole time? It felt weird to think he might have been watching me sleep.

"Don't worry I haven't been here the whole time," he said as if he could read my mind. "I just sporadically check it throughout the day."

The wind flapped the loose corner of the canvas open every so often, allowing me to look outside from where I lay. The sun was still high in the sky, confusing me. Was it day or night?

"Your turn," Calvin said and passed me the long metal fire poker the second I sat up. "See you in the morning." He didn't seem to want to make small talk and that suited me just fine.

I watched him duck out. Unlike me, he had a home to go back to. I wondered what kind of trouble he'd gotten himself into to have to be here.

I put a few more logs on the fire for safe measure before walking over to the slow-moving river a mere minute away to splash cold water on my face. An old man was fishing, wading up to his knees. He was so still I almost didn't see him.

On my way back to the teepee, I saw a long lineup of people outside the band office. The line was so long it turned at the bend of the road until I couldn't see the end of it. I hoped it wasn't a lineup for the outhouse, or else I'd have to squat in the bushes.

"What's everyone lined up for?" I asked Calvin when I spotted him near our tent. He had come back to grab something he forgot.

"They're electing a new Chief."

"What's wrong with the one they got?" I asked.

"Nothing. She's a good Chief, but they have an election every four years just like the government, and the new guy running against Cayenne is corrupt. At least Cayenne cares about the people. Most of them are only in it for the money."

"Oh." I shook my head and poked the fire, trying to understand the politics.

Just then a mouse scurried out from under his bag. "Listen. You can't leave food lying around in the tent; the mice are starting to come around. Feed it to the fire if you're not going to finish it," he said.

"Feed?"

"Yeah. Feeding food to the fire is a gift to the spirits, to our Ancestors. They're our family. They need to be nourished, too, and acknowledged. The fire opens a doorway to communicate with the ones who have gone before us."

I didn't say anything. After witnessing the wreckage that fire could leave behind, I didn't think it could ever bring about anything good.

Later that evening, I walked past the dwindling lineup and noticed it was mostly middle-aged women. The polls were open all day, and it was down to Cayenne and two other male candidates. I didn't hear the speeches that were taking place inside the gym, but I heard the musings outside.

"I hope she wins," said one woman to another.

"Someone said they tried using bad medicine on her."

"She never slept a wink last night. There were dozens of rodents running around her house all night. She had to set traps this morning."

Despite the rumours that she might lose, the next day it was announced that Cayenne would remain Chief. The news caused much relief in the cheering crowd who couldn't fit inside the band office where the announcement was made.

Speeches outside the band office honoured Cayenne as a leader who selflessly gave her time and energy to the community and helped ensure cultural traditions continued on, including the job of Firekeeper. The crowd looked over at me and Calvin and applauded. I stood there feeling out of place.

There was a Drum Dance outside the teepee that night and everyone danced in a circle, stomping to the beat of the drums until the ground shook. I watched from the tent, too embarrassed to join.

"Aren't you going to join us?" Cayenne said as she peeked her head into the teepee.

"I don't know how."

"It's really easy, just put one foot in front of the other,"

"Congratulations," I said.

"Thanks."

"Is it only the men who are allowed to sing and drum?" I asked as one of the Elders belted out a powerful wail in the middle of the song, encouraging the other drummers to sing louder.

"It didn't always used to be that way. Women used to drum too, before the Indian Act took away our rights."

"Oh?" More politics that I didn't understand.

She whispered, "All it comes down to is, we're too powerful."

"Oh?" I said again, not sure of what she meant.

"We're the life givers. The drum is the heartbeat. Come on."

She took my hand and pulled me up, then ushered me into the circle. As reluctant as I was, I put one foot in front of the other like she said. Cayenne saw that I was looking around at everyone else's feet to follow along.

"You ever heard the expression 'march to the beat of your own drum'? Close your eyes and let the music guide you. Each of us has a different path, a different relationship with Creator. The way you dance in the circle is different than anyone else."

I let myself feel the steady drumbeat course through my chest, listening to the cries of the singers. Their songs had meaning, each one had a message. Even though I couldn't understand the language, I knew each song was strikingly different.

When the dance was finally over, it felt like time had stopped. That's when I panicked.

The fire.

I ran back to the teepee, hoping the flame hadn't died out. How long had I been dancing? I felt like I had fallen into a trance. To my relief, the fire was still burning. I could see the flames wavering in the shadows through the teepee canvas.

I plunked down next to the fire in a sweat and felt the warm, smooth rocks. They matched the feeling I had inside me. It was a feeling I didn't know what to do with. The warmth in the centre between my ribs was so unfamiliar that I didn't know if it was uncomfortable or soothing.

When I woke the next day, not a soul was in sight. Tables and chairs had been taken down outside the band office and out of the rain. Other than the evidence of footprints in the mud forming a circle in the field, it looked like no one had been there at all the night before.

Calvin came in and made a long, drawn-out sound as he yawned and stretched at the same time. He held off on pouring the bucket of water over the fire until I packed the few things I had with me. We stood and watched as the fire finally sizzled out, filling the teepee with thick smoke.

Those three days had gone by fast. Looking back, it could very well have been a dream. Sleeping on the ground next to the fire had grounded me in a way that I never knew I needed, but when my firekeeping services were no longer required, that familiar empty feeling crept back in. What would I do now? Where would I go?

I knew one thing for sure — I wanted to be of service. I needed to be of service. It gave me a sense of fulfillment I never felt before. I walked to the band office to see if Cayenne might have any more jobs for me.

The band office was empty except for a few children huddled on an old couch watching cartoons on a small TV. Cayenne was nowhere to be found.

I didn't know what else to do so I just sat outside on the steps and waited. When Cayenne came around the corner, I was slumped over on the steps playing with a twig, watching the ants work as they marched past my feet.

"There you are. I was looking for you. Come, I'll show you where you're going to stay." She drove me on her four-wheeler to an old camper that was parked at a campsite on the outskirts of the reserve.

"There's electricity, but you'll have to use the shared public washrooms and cook over an open fire," Cayenne walked me through the camper as she talked. "This is where you'll stay for the next little while. Don't worry, it has a built-in heater for when the nights start getting colder. I'm just up the road if you need me. Across from the band office, the house with the marijuana flag in the window. Don't ask, it's my son's," she laughed. "Tomorrow, I'll pick you up and bring you to one of the Elders. Her name's Alice. She's a well-known healer in the community. The court asked us to pair you with a mentor, but around here we call her Auntie Alice." She smiled.

"Okay."

"And don't be shy to let me know if you need anything. The fridge is stocked, just make sure to lock this door. If you hear any noises outside, it could be a bear, but they usually don't come too close to the reserve unless they smell food. So keep any food you have contained. Just in case, there's bear bangers in the drawer by the sink. All good?"

I nodded again, "I think so."

I was glad to see Cayenne's friendly face the next morning when she picked me up to bring me up the road to see Alice.

When Alice opened the door with a welcoming smile, I felt at ease. Alice's husband sat in the living room watching old western shows with the volume on low. I sat quietly trying to be polite.

"This coming summer will be hard for the community," Alice started.

"Oh, how so?" Cayenne asked as she sipped the tea Alice poured both of us without asking if we wanted it.

"We will need lots of rain. When they took the oil out of the ground, it separated the earth. The water fell deep down. The ground way underneath soaked it all up. The earth is thirsty. Down south, they've been taking too much oil out of the ground for too long. Just like when I'm baking, oil and water don't mix. When I make my bannock, I pour water into a cup and when I pour oil in, the water sinks to the bottom and the oil sits on top. Well, it's the same when they take out the oil from the ground. The water falls down, down, down, and the earth gets dry. This summer will be too dry. And we will see something we never seen in our lifetime. It's a … what do you call it? A sequence of what they did."

"Consequence?" Cayenne guessed.

"Yes, consequence. You and your fancy words, you young people," she laughed. "If the summer fires make it to the old, abandoned mine, that poison will go into the ground. It will destroy everything in its path, all the way out to the Arctic Ocean."

Cayenne looked down and shook her head. "They need to do something about that mine. It's awful."

I had some inkling of what they were talking about when they mentioned the gold mine. I had been in the emergency room for a head injury when an explosion happened at the mine. That day, I was jumping on Em's bed when we were both still quite young. I fell off and hit my head on the corner of her dresser. My head split open just above my eyebrow.

Not able to get a hold of my mom, Em called her dad and he came home from work and rushed me to the hospital. I remember the wait to see the doctor being so long. Em's dad left me alone there after he got called back to work. The nurses tried and tried to get a hold of my mom, and when they finally did she arrived in a cab. She was half-cut and angry that I'd hurt myself.

"What happened to you? You're so clumsy."

"I fell."

She mumbled something about the hospital being the last place she wanted to be while we waited for the doctor. Then suddenly, the hospital turned into a frenzy. Stretchers were wheeled quickly into the emergency room until there was no space left to keep injured patients.

"What's going on?" My mom stopped one of the nurses in the hallway.

"There's been an explosion at the mine."

"Well, does she need stitches or not?" my mom asked impatiently. The nurse took a quick second to look at my head after my mom had swatted my hand away to let her inspect the wound. I was relieved to put my arm down as I'd been holding a towel up to the wound to stop the bleeding the entire time.

"I can't be the one to tell you that. You can either wait to see the doctor or take your chances," she said.

"I'll take my chances," my mom said; she grabbed me by the arm and brought me home in a cab. The small butterfly bandage the nurses put over the deep gash before I left the hospital didn't stay on for very long and the wound didn't heal properly, leaving a keloid scar. On the news I found out that nine people died that day. All I could think about was how my mom probably wished I was the tenth.

"There's enough poison in there to kill the world twice over," Alice's husband piped in out of the blue.

He'd been watching TV but muted the volume when he heard the word mine.

"Alfred's had his share of mining catastrophes. He was forced into bagging uranium for the atomic bomb back when he was a boy. He didn't know it would eventually cause most everyone he knew to fall ill with cancer and die well before their time," Alice said as Alfred closed his eyes in sadness.

"He often questions how he escaped the sickness himself," Alice said quietly.

I sat and listened as they went on about the mining industry and the devastation it caused to the land and to their health throughout their lifetime.

"Look at those trees; they're falling all over the place. The permafrost is melting now too. Drunken trees we call them." Alice pointed out the window at a cluster of tall birch trees that looked like they'd been blown over by a giant.

"I almost forgot. Alice, this is Nyla. She's one of our community helpers. She'll be living out at the campsite for a little while. The courts asked if you could be someone she can talk to," Cayenne said.

"Is she from here?" Alice asked Cayenne, as if I couldn't understand English.

"She's not from here, but she's done good work for us. She was one of our Firekeepers during the election." Cayenne smiled at me proudly. "Nyla, where are you from?" she asked.

I felt self-conscious and shifted in my seat. "I, um … I don't remember. I moved to Coppertown when I was young. So, I guess I'm from there."

"So it was just you and your mother growing up?" Alice guessed.

I nodded. "I moved out when I was young," I said, without batting an eye.

"That must have been hard for you. How did you get by?"

I shrugged my shoulders, "I'm not sure." I could feel the sting of tears. No one had ever asked me what it was like having to get by on my own.

"Let's go for a walk, hmm?" Alice said, saving me from crying in front of Cayenne and Alfred, who sat and watched cowboys gun fighting until we returned.

I followed Alice down to the edge of the river, where the migrating pelicans bathed and floated in the murky, coffee-cream swirls of current that stirred up sediment from the silky mud bottom.

"I come here when I need to breathe. To remind myself that my sorrows can be washed away like the water that floats down the river. The river carries away all my troubles." Alice paused. "So, what happened for you to be here and what makes you think you are so bad?"

How did she know? Was it that obvious how I felt? Her seemingly non-judgemental nature made it easier for me to open up to her.

"I did something really stupid. I've done things that I can't take back even if I wanted to."

"Yes, but things have been done to you too, no?"

I shrugged again, "I guess." Tears filled my eyes, but I tried hard to keep them from falling. I didn't want to feel sorry for myself.

"It's okay to cry. Your tears can help heal you," she said softly. "Water is what heals us. It can put out the fire that rages within us."

I looked up at her wide-eyed. She knew.

"You need to go to the water, my dear."

And just like that, my tears ran like the river before me.

≈

EIGHT

There were five of us piled into the metal boat with a canopy and two engines, one for backup. I didn't know anyone except Alice. The others were camp helpers. The driver, Sizeh, lifted the engines and took it slow as we navigated through the swampy shallow areas. I quickly lost my sense of direction, with no idea where we were going other than being told we were going to a place called the Thousand Islands.

We passed by a small reef that Alice said was usually hidden under water, where only glimpses of it could be seen on windy days.

"Ever since the water started getting low, we can see it all the time." She pointed ahead towards the reef.

Once we turned the corner, I saw the islands dotting the expanse of water and we began to make our way through the maze.

Alice was no stranger to the islands. "My family has travelled these waters for thousands of years. I used to live out here after my parents took us and ran into the bush when the missionaries came. They couldn't find us out here."

She could see I looked puzzled by what she meant. "Do you know about the missionaries?" she asked.

I shook my head.

"They took the children and made them go to residential school. They probably made your parents go, too. Lots of people are hurting now because of what the residential schools did to us. It will take many generations for our people to heal."

I stared down into the water where a rainbow formed through the spraying mist, refracting light at just the right angle. I stared until an old memory stirred within me. My mom was on the phone with my aunt talking about having to travel somewhere to go to school when they were young. They had to be away from their parents. Maybe that's why my mom was never close to them, I thought.

Maybe that's why she was never close to me.

I pushed the notion away. Imagining my mother as a scared little girl made me feel sorry for her, but I didn't want to feel pity for her.

I closed my eyes and for a moment I saw my mother's rare smile. It was a still image like a photograph in my mind: I had made her smile once. She was watching me from the window as I tried to catch a butterfly when, to my surprise, it landed on my nose. I went cross-eyed for a moment, trying to get a good look at it up close and I could hear her laugh. As it flew away, I caught a glimpse of her amusement just before she shut the curtain.

I turned towards the water and let the wind off the lake take my tears.

Alice sat quietly in her purple windbreaker jacket. The wind tossed the loose edges of her flower-print scarf, which she had wrapped around her head and tied in a bow under her chin to protect her ears from the wind and keep her short hair tidy. A healthy amount of hairspray in her bangs held them up high in the front with a barrette.

After a few hours of steady navigation through the islands, with only the sound of the boat crashing against the water and the engine revving and slowing on each turn, the boat came upon the shoreline of what looked like a small, abandoned village.

"Here we are," Alice said.

Sizeh helped me and the others out of the boat after helping Alice, and it took me a moment to get my footing on the rickety dock. I looked into the water to see a large white bubble.

"That's a moose hide. We're soaking it to make it soft," Alice said.

There were people there to greet us when we docked; most

everyone was busy doing something. A group of what I'd heard the Elders around the fire call "yout," who looked a few years younger than me, were camping out for the weekend to finish a video project about the importance of being out on the land.

The Elders sat under a shiny blue tarp that served as a shelter from the wind, set up on a slant above the fire and held in place with teepee poles. A grumpy-looking woman with one hand on her hip flipped pieces of charred meat and fish on the grill.

"Come." One of the Elders called me over to sit beside him. I walked over to him feeling self-conscious and plunked myself down beside him on a log that served as a chair, and the smoke from the fire instantly gravitated towards me.

"White rabbits," one of the Elders laughed as I got up to move away from the smoke. "Say 'go away white rabbits.'"

I wasn't sure if he was joking.

"Go on. They'll go away," he encouraged.

"Go away white rabbits," I said, feeling silly, but just like that the smoke drifted away from me.

"See, I told you!" He gave me a toothless grin.

"Nyla," Alice called out to me from the small shed where people were washing dishes in a basin on the steps. "Let's go for a walk."

We walked side by side to the end of the trail, where she stopped abruptly and held my hand so I could help keep her balance on the unsteady ground.

"Do you see these rocks?"

There at our feet was a large circle of rocks, each of them the size of my head.

"You're standing in a place where there was once a teepee. These rocks were used to hold it down. It looks like the kids moved them out of the way when they were shooting their video. They don't know there's a history here. They're pointing that camera every which way trying to find something. Well, it's right here." She rolled one of the rocks back into its imprint in the ground.

"I wouldn't have known either," I said. "I would have walked by and thought nothing of it."

"We walk by important things every day that we don't see with our eyes." She pointed to her eyes for added effect. "Let's keep walking. There's lots to see," she said and closed her eyes tight, making a funny face to try and make me smile. It worked.

"Do you see these small boulders here in a line?" she asked when we got to a slope of smooth rock next to the shore.

"Yes." They were the same size as the ones we just passed.

"Do you know what they were once used for?" she quizzed me.

"Another teepee?" It was my best guess.

"A canoe," she corrected. "There was a time when we made our own canoes out of birch bark. We would place these heavy rocks in the bottom to make sure it was nice and flat." She tried to lift one but changed her mind. "Too heavy for me in my old age."

She looked up at me. "Everything has a purpose. Even an old stone. Even an old lady." She laughed.

She kept walking, and I followed her into the trees until she stopped in front of a bush full of orange berries that looked like raspberries.

"Try one."

I picked a few off the branch and was about to put them into my mouth when I saw a small green worm inside one.

I threw the berry on the ground.

Alice looked at me curiously. "Why be scared of a worm? It can't hurt you."

My face turned red.

As we continued to walk, I pulled one of the berries apart and ate it slowly while inspecting it for another worm, careful not to crush it in my fingers. I didn't want to eat them, but I knew wasting them would displease Alice.

We walked around the lake to where on a balmy day the water hit the rocks violently; there was nothing to be seen for miles, just open water. The lake was so big that it looked like an endless ocean. I saw a large piece of plywood on the ground. It didn't lay quite flat and looked to be covering something.

"This is what I brought you here for. Go ahead, lift it up," Alice instructed.

I reached down and lifted the wobbly sheet of plywood — only to unexpectedly find myself back in my old apartment, lifting the lid of the crawl space I used to hide in.

I let go and fell back, landing on the palms of my hands on the hard rock.

"I can't," I said, suddenly overwhelmed with the vivid sensation of being a child again. The smells, the sounds, the fear. "What just happened?"

"It's all right. I'm right here. Do you want me to help you lift it?"

I shook my head, staring at the plywood. "I don't want to lift it. Why do you want me to lift it?" A part of me wanted to be brave, but another part of me wanted to run. The plywood was light; the weight of it wasn't the problem. It was the weight of the fear of what I would find underneath it that held me back.

"You know why Nyla. I don't need to tell you why. Go on, it's okay. I'm right here," she said and pointed at her eyes again. "There's more than meets the eye."

This time when I lifted it, all I saw was darkness. The shadows brought me back to the oil-soaked plywood at the old cemetery. Black sticky tar covered my hands and I could smell the fumes.

I dropped the board again and looked at my hands. They were smooth except for the few pebbles indented into my skin from falling backwards and catching myself.

It was so real. I was right there. "What's happening to me?"

"You're seeing visions, Nyla. It's okay. It happens to some of us when we begin our healing journey. Try again. This time try to see beyond the memories."

"I can't."

"What is it you're afraid of?"

"I don't want to go back there. I thought healing meant looking ahead, not into the past?"

"You cannot carry your burden with you wherever you go. You must put it down. It is too heavy. Lay it to rest. You can't bring unresolved hurt with you. Face it. Don't run from it."

Somehow, on an intrinsic level, I knew she was right. I nodded. Although still afraid, I knelt back down and Alice helped me lift the plywood. I closed my eyes; when I opened them, before me was a large, empty hole in the rock. No memories, just the present moment.

"What is it?" I asked.

"This is where you must bathe."

"Bathe?" I asked.

"Yes. You must follow the original instructions of this place, the ones that are not written."

The hole in the rock was perfectly round and smooth, as if a sphere had fallen to earth from space.

"Not everyone knows about this, and we must keep it that way. It is only for those who require healing. There are many of these pools, and they have been used by our Ancestors for thousands of years. They are lined up all along the Thousand Islands, up to the Old Lady of the Falls. You will go there when you are ready. Not just anyone can go to visit, and when you do, you must first have cleansed your mind, body, and heart."

"But there's no water in it."

"Not yet. You must wait."

"Wait for what?"

"For the rain." She looked up and held her opened palms up to the sky.

"How did the rock form this way, anyway?" I asked as I tried to work through my fear.

"The Sky Spirits. You can see them dancing on cold clear nights," she said, looking up.

"You mean the Northern Lights?"
"Yes, they are our Ancestors."

That evening I slept in a large canvas tent set up a few feet above ground on a wooden platform. Next to it sat Alice's tent so I felt safe. Before retreating for the night I looked up at the stars over the water. The night bordered somewhere between light and darkness. The trees looked so small on the scattered islands laid out in front of me, but after a while they started to look like hundreds of tall people standing still and watching me from a distance.

I looked away for fear that my mind was playing tricks on me. At any moment they might move and make their way toward me, crashing through the water. Even the stars began to look strange. They seemed to be getting closer and closer.

Then they started to align in formation.

The world was silent as the suspended orbs peacefully floated in a perfect line, bobbing through the night sky as if floating in the water, their reflection bouncing off the waves. There was nothing chaotic about them, but as they came closer, I retreated into the tent without taking my eyes off them.

They eventually nestled slowly into the tree line on one of the thousand islands in front of me.

Then, one by one, the trees caught fire like a row of candles on a birthday cake. The northern fire season had begun. The pools of healing water would have to wait.

～

NINE

On the way back to the reserve the next morning the fire followed us. A black cloud rose from the horizon behind us like a monster chasing its prey until it covered the sun and swallowed it whole. The day turned into night in a matter of seconds. People in the community came out of their houses to see what had caused the sky to become dark in the middle of the day.

I stared in awe at the red lightning that flashed in the sky as the black wall of smoke spewed down rain and ash. Cayenne came running up to me. "Come on. Get inside."

Mothers ran outside to grab their kids, who had been playing kick the can in the middle of the road. Everyone shut their windows and doors. "It's the bloody end of the world," Cayenne said. "Hurry." She grabbed my things from the dock and threw them into the back of her four-wheeler.

"The fire swept through the cut lines," a man said to Cayenne from outside her house just as we stepped inside. "They just blocked the road. Nobody's getting in or out. It jumped the damn highway. We're going to need a lot more hands."

Cayenne looked over at me. "Right here."

"Me?" I said in surprise.

"Yes. You can help the guys fill up the water buckets until the planes get here. Don't worry, they'll take care of you."

Mav was the community's fire chief. His real name was Maverick, but everyone called him Mav. It was obvious that he was Cayenne's brother; they could pass as twins, their features were so similar. Mav drove me and a few other stragglers he had recruited from around the reserve down to the warehouse in his rusty pick-up truck in a mad hurry. It would be our job to fend off the fire until the experts showed up.

At a big warehouse just outside the community that housed all kinds of equipment, at least a dozen guys were already suited up in yellow jumpsuits, walking up and down the road with heavy packs on their backs and doing squats every few steps.

"They've been preparing for this all summer," Mav said. Still, they looked like a real haphazard bunch and me being added to the mix didn't make them look any better.

"Boss, they're stopping traffic. Tankers too. The reserve's surrounded in flames," one guy said to Mav through the driver's side window before Mav could even open the door of the truck. SUP was spelled out in bold capital letters on a white label sewed onto his overalls above his chest pocket. I thought it said "soup" at first, but later he told me it was short for supervisor and it became his nickname among the crew.

"I brought a few more hands," Mav said to Sup.

Just then a small airplane flew over the lake and dropped a red, thick powder on the other side of the riverbank, where the flames looked like mini tornadoes.

"What is that?" I asked.

"Flame retardant."

"The fire's creating its own storm," Mav said as he pointed at the low, crackling lightning that changed to a thunderous roar every few minutes.

Just then Cayenne showed up on her four-wheeler. She was in such a flurry she drove it without sitting down. "I called some of the other communities. They're pulling their crews together and coming across by boat. We'll have to put everyone up in the lodge. The rest of us might have to evacuate."

"Let's get to work boys," Sup said, then looked at me. "And lady!" he added, tossing me a pair of tarnished overalls. "Here, put these on and start filling those water buckets over there."

I did as I was told and geared up where I stood, pulling the used overalls over my clothes. For the remainder of the day, I couldn't fill up the buckets fast enough even though I never once took a break.

That night I shared a room in the lodge with another firefighter, one of the professionals they sent in from the other side of the country. The hotel staff set up cots in the restaurant and hallways because there weren't enough beds for the firefighters.

It wasn't weird for me having to sleep in a room with a total stranger; I had become used to it. Unlike Charmaine, this roommate didn't talk much. She was visibly exhausted from fighting fires.

"I haven't slept in days," she said as she sat at the foot of the bed closest to the window and struggled to take her damp, sweaty socks off. Soot covered her entire face. The next thing I knew she was out cold.

The sky stayed dark for three days, raining ash that left everything it touched smeared in soot. The fire moved in on the community fast, and desperation set in. With no road left, children and Elders were being evacuated by helicopter. Those fit enough stayed behind to fight until the beast was put to rest.

The band office served as the emergency meet-up spot, and it was stocked with supplies. I stopped in for a quick break in between filling water buckets.

The cleansing pool was beginning to feel like an imaginary oasis.

Mav walked into the band office just as I was walking out. "Nyla, How do you feel about going out on the front lines?"

"Good," I said. I was ready to do whatever it took. Fire had become my familiar adversary, and it was about time I gave it a good fight.

"People gotta start butting out their damn cigarettes," Sup told Mav when we got to the warehouse.

"You think that's what started this one?"

"Who knows. It's been bone dry."

I was just glad that this time it wasn't my fault.

I followed Mav's orders and started clearing the brush around the cabins on the outskirts of the reserve. We hosed the cabins down with water from the small pond. My feet were scorching, and I wasn't even anywhere near the fire. The fire was so strong, it flowed underground, making the earth hot to the touch.

Out there in the field, I was uncertain of where to step. A flame could spring up anywhere. It had been so dry that summer that the trickle of rain that did come down couldn't put the fire out. Firestorm lightning would just start more small fires that joined in with the larger fire.

Once we did all we could do around the perimeter of the cabins, Mav drove us down the old dirt road, the only road leading out of the reserve. We went as far as we could before he started to worry about the engine getting too hot. When we could no longer see the road through the thick smoke, we turned around. About halfway back to the reserve, he dropped us off.

"I'll be back to pick you up in a couple hours. Be safe out there," he said and reversed, skidding his tires in the ditch and kicking up large chunks of gravel when he turned around.

"Follow me," said Sup to the rest of us.

We walked through the trees on the other side of the road where the fire hadn't crossed and trudged over rocks through thick brush. I swatted mosquitoes and dusted off the sticky spiderwebs I walked into. Sup seemed unphased by the inhospitable surroundings.

"None of this would have happened if they just let us continue our cultural burning practices," he muttered.

"Cultural burning?"

"It's what we used to do before the white man showed up and told us we weren't allowed to do anything for ourselves anymore. We used to back burn the trees and dig trenches so the fires wouldn't get this out of hand."

"Can't you bring it back?" It seemed like the obvious solution.

"I guess that's sorta what we're doing now, but we need to be more proactive and not so reactive," he said, stopping in his tracks next to a wooden spray-painted stake where another crew was already hard at work, all of them evenly spread arms-length apart.

"Start here and work your way north," he pointed to where I could only guess north was. "Just follow these ruffians," he joked. The crew took full advantage of the informal introduction as a reason to take a break. Each of them took a big swig of water from the large jug they shared.

It felt like what I imagined a war zone to be. They all carried weapons — axes, shovels, and chainsaws.

For the most part we weren't putting the fire out with water, as I assumed would have been the case. We were attacking it at its root to snuff it out as it smouldered under our feet, melting the rubber under our steel toe boots.

I could faintly hear Sup over the sound of burning tinder cracking and falling in the distance. "The wind's blowing to the west, turning the fire back on itself. It can change course any minute," he yelled as he worked fervently to my left.

Gusts of wind whipped the fire around into dancing flames, then settled again as it burned steadily at the cut line. Fire was always unpredictable. Small flames popped up at my feet and I stabbed at the ground relentlessly to put them out. It was satisfying to see the fire retreat back into the ground until it found another way out from under another mound of dry soil and brush a few feet away. I ran to each small fire and attacked them like a game of whack-a-mole.

It was sweaty, gruelling work, but I never stopped once for a rest even when everyone else did. I was obsessed, compulsive. Anyone would think I had a personal vendetta. In a way, I did.

I was so focused, I didn't hear Sup yell and was shocked when he yanked me aside to make room for the herd of caribou that appeared by the hundreds, fleeing for their lives. They burst out of the forest in front of us in droves as we all jumped out of the way before they trampled us. The dispossessed herd galloped past us in zigs zags, jumping over whatever was in their way.

In the coming days, bears, moose, lynx, wolverines, bison, foxes and rabbits came out from the safety of their dens. They ran straight past us with fear in their eyes, their homes ablaze.

At first, I feared them. I thought they might try to attack, but then I realized they were relying on us to help them. I heard it in their cries. Even the most formidable creatures in the forest were at the mercy of the fire except for an immortal breed of fire bug, an insect with two stingers that made their nests in the burned stumps. They were so indestructible, "they could only have come directly from the pit of hell," said Sup, joking that they would later haunt him in his dreams.

It was a wonder that we were able to fend off the fire from coming too close to us while we were out there on the line, but we somehow managed to stave it off for another day. As the night neared, the fire slowed down without heat from the sun giving it energy. Almost as if it went to sleep in a steady burn until the morning.

On the drive back to the warehouse after a hard day's work, we were all noticeably exhausted. None of us had the energy to move a muscle. Some of the crew fell fast asleep, their heads bobbing every time we hit a bump. The embers in the air above us were an eerie reminder that our work was far from over.

"Sup, pull over man. I gotta take a leak," said one of the guys in the back seat.

A few of the guys got out and went around the truck to do their business, then suddenly one of them yelled, "Hey, you all right, man?"

Sup jumped out of the truck and I looked in the rearview from shotgun to see what the problem was. One of the bigger guys on the crew, Ricky, was lying flat on the ground on his back.

"He was just standing there swaying and then fell straight backwards," said Archie. His name was the easiest to remember because he was the only redheaded Native on the reserve. I wasn't sure if Archie was even his real name or if people just started calling him that after the comic book character.

Sup ran to Ricky and sat him up. "Nyla, bring the water," he yelled.

I grabbed the big jug of water sitting on the middle console and ran it over. "He's dehydrated. Too much sun. Too much heat. How long's he been like this?"

"He was slurring his words a bit," said Archie. "I thought he was joking, or maybe snuck a couple swigs of that mickey he was carrying around the other day."

Ricky still didn't come to even after Sup splashed him with water and wet his lips, but he was still breathing.

"We gotta get him to the hospital."

We all struggled to pick him up and load him into the truck. He was completely comatose as he lay in the back seat across our laps. We rolled all the windows down for fresh air even though the cab filled with more smoke than air. Sup radioed for help, and the helicopter was already at the lodge waiting to medivac Ricky to Coppertown by the time we got there.

I learned a few days later that Ricky had suffered heatstroke from overexertion. But once he got his fluids up, he was right back out on the line with the rest of us like he never missed a beat.

"Good work out there," Mav said to the crew at the end of a hard week. In the gym next to the band office, we were seated at a long table made out of smaller folding tables. We gobbled down our food, famished. No one talked about what happened to Ricky so as not to embarrass him.

The next day, I geared up groggily after a solid few hours of sleep. Just as I was about to hop into Mav's truck, Sup approached me.

"The fire's moving in fast. We think there might be a few families trapped at their cabins. We need someone smaller, more agile, that we can lower out of the helicopter to help get them out of there. You up for it?"

"Yes," I said without hesitation.

The land from above was spectacular. I could see the curve of the earth. The ground was ravished with hundreds of fires like dropped bombs, their smoke blending in with the clouds. I watched them grow larger and build momentum as they joined forces.

The pilot spoke into the microphone. "Looks like a battlefield."

When we spotted a small, log cabin surrounded by smoke and flames, we circled sideways a few times until we got close enough without hitting the trees.

"You're not scared of heights, are ya?" the pilot asked through his scratchy microphone.

I shrugged.

"Was it a coin toss?"

"She's got no fear, not like these guys," Sup answered for me as he nudged the two big lugs on either side of him.

When we spotted a helpless family waving their arms in the air, the pilot lowered the helicopter so close I could see their tear-stained cheeks.

"Mom and baby first," Sup said as he lowered the ladder.

As unsure as I was about hanging out of a helicopter, I had more concern for the family than for myself. Sup hooked me up to a hoist with a harness and a quick release in case I lost my grip on the swaying ladder.

"She's got smoke in her lungs. She won't stop screaming!" The mother cried once my feet touched the ground.

"We need to put her on your back so you can climb up," I yelled over the sound of the chopper. The mother carefully handed the baby over to her husband and the baby's head flung back in a wail. I quickly unravelled the blanket the baby was swaddled in and tied it in a criss-cross around the mother's chest and waist. The baby fit snug inside the blanket on her back, and I tightened the front until it was secure.

The mom stepped into the harness and held one hand on the baby's bottom to help hold her up, worried she might fall out.

"You go first." I held the ladder steady as the mom began to pull herself up, noticeably afraid to leave the rest of her children and husband behind. Mav and Sup lay on their stomachs on each side of the ladder, ready to pull her in when she got close enough. But halfway up she froze in fear. "Don't look down," I instructed when I saw her look behind me at her family. "It's okay. They're right behind you." She started shaking.

"Keep going." I gently pushed on the bottom of her feet to encourage her to take another step.

Mav reached for her hand, but she was too afraid to let go of the rope. Just then a gust of wind forced the helicopter to swerve. "Mom!" one of the children cried. She screamed and let one hand go of the ladder to reach for her baby.

"Don't let go. You're not going to fall," I said calmly.

The woman took one more brave step and was finally lifted into the helicopter, where she held her baby tight, rocking back and forth.

I hurried back down the ladder and helped the other two children put harnesses on and get their footing on the ladder. One by one, the family made their way up. As we closed the helicopter doors and flew to safety, the father stared blankly at his cabin, all his hard work over the years gone in a blink of an eye.

That night, the crew delved into a smorgasbord of food like a pack of wild animals.

Sup stood up and clinked his drink, "To Nyla. You're a hero!" he cheered.

The rest of the crew banged on the table with both hands, some with bannock stuffed in their mouths, chanting, "Speech, speech, speech!"

My cheeks flushed red.

"Stand up and take a bow," Sup insisted.

They all clapped wildly and whistled when I slowly rose into a half-stand leaning my hands on the table and trying to hide my face behind my hair. Sup howled like a dog.

I couldn't help but laugh. I wanted to be happy. It felt possible. But I wouldn't let myself go there — I was an imposter. If they knew who I really was, knew what I'd done, would they still think of me as a hero?

~

It was the summer of the apocalypse, but together our small fire crew managed to save the reserve from burning down. I had more than completed my community service work. With the fire season officially over, I dreaded the moment when Cayenne would tell me I was free to go.

Fear of having to leave loomed over me. Where was I to go? I didn't want to go back to Coppertown. There was nothing there for me. At least on the reserve, I had people who seemed to care about me.

When I saw Cayenne, she told me what I already knew. "Well you seem to have exceeded your community service hours; your probation officer will be pleased." My sullen look must have been obvious because she followed up with, "Do you have anywhere to go? Any family back in Coppertown?"

I just shook my head and looked down shamefully.

She must have already suspected that was the case because she said, "You know you never did get a chance to finish the work you were doing with Alice, and I could always use some extra help around here setting up for feasts and Drum Dances."

I felt a jolt of excitement wash over me. Was this what happiness felt like?

"Thank you, Cayenne," I said in humble gratitude.

I continued to live out of the old camper through the fall and winter, and Alice invited me out to her bush camp when the lake froze. Nothing about bush camp was easy. It wasn't even easy getting there. The skidoo ride took eight hours and by the time we got there

I was so flush with the cold air hitting my face, I fell into a deep sleep and forgot where I was when I woke up.

There was always something to do at bush camp. There were only a handful of us. Alice and Alfred brought some of the troubled youth out there regularly, and together we cycled through the chores. One day I swept the old wood floors and cleaned the counters of the large cabin that was also sometimes used as a tourist destination. The next day I'd be outside chopping wood or picking spruce boughs to lay down on the ground inside my canvas tent. Although the cabin had all the amenities one would need, we slept outside in the cold in tents, each one equipped with its own wood stove.

The mornings were hardest. To get up cold and tend to the fire was demanding and dreadful at the same time. The days were long as we scraped hides and sat outside around the fire looking out at the frozen lake, talking about the weather when we had a moment in between chores.

One day as we all stood around the fire at the shoreline, making bannock on a stick for lunch, I saw something dart across the lake.

"Wolverine!" someone yelled.

George, our hunting guide, ran for his gun. He aimed and shot but missed, scaring the wolverine into a scurry and making it drop its kill, a small white rabbit. Not wanting to leave it behind, the wolverine stood in limbo for a moment, almost as if it was contemplating the risk. Would it go back for its kill? Or leave it behind and run to safety?

When George shot his gun again, the wolverine thought better of it and ran, leaving the ravens to scavenge its dinner.

"It'll come back no doubt. Keep an eye out for it. Now that it knows there's food nearby it'll be coming back," George warned. "Would've made a nice pair of mitts," he said and shook his head.

Sure enough, the wolverine did come back. I only smelled it at first but didn't know where the intense odour was coming from. Later on, George told me they are like skunks, secreting a strong scent to mark their territory and keep predators away. I wondered then if my spirit animal might be a wolverine. I thought of my aunt.

I saw the animal from the corner of my eye that evening as I sat at the fire but didn't tell anyone. It deserved a second chance. Don't we all?

In my down time, I tried skiing but couldn't coordinate myself enough to glide across the deeply grooved ski trails. I tried skating, but the skates were so tight they hurt my feet. So instead of taking up an activity like everyone else, when I was done my chores, I just sat around the fire on an old plastic chair, alone, staring into the flames and sipping hot chocolate. Every so often, someone would come sit around the fire with me and smoke. I no longer had the desire to smoke. I could never really stand the smell of it to begin with.

Alice came around one evening and sat down across from me at the fire. "Everyone's inside playing cards."

"I don't really play cards," I said. It reminded me too much of being in jail, but she didn't need to know that.

"You're not cold?"

"Not really, no." I got up to put another log on the fire, seeing she was shivering a bit.

"Here," she said, taking out a shawl from the inside of her jacket. "At least put this on over your head. It's windy. The wind will get into your ears and you'll catch a cold."

Did she come out here just to give me this? Because she was so caring, I put it on to appease her but felt far too young to be wearing a granny scarf.

"The fire is very spiritual for us, you know. It connects us to the spirit world." She pulled out a package of fresh tobacco from inside the sleeve of her jacket.

What else was she hiding in that jacket?

"That is why we feed the fire." She got up and sprinkled tobacco into the fire and closed her eyes for quite some time.

I didn't know what to do so I stood up and closed my eyes too, so as not to be rude.

After a time, she said, "You can open your eyes now, Nyla."

I opened them and noticed the brightness of the moon shining down on us.

"Who did you pray for?"

"Um, I don't really know how to pray," I said feeling slightly ashamed.

"That's okay, you will learn over time. You know who I prayed for? I prayed for you. I asked our Ancestors to watch over you, to help you on your journey."

Alice had such a way of making me feel special.

She walked over to me on the other side of the fire. "Open your hand." I did as I was told, and she put a small pinch of tobacco in my palm. "Try again."

I closed my eyes, gently tossing the tobacco into the fire and listening to it crackle.

"Who do you see?"

I searched my mind and saw my mother's face when the doctor told her she had liver disease. I saw Noah's expression inside the burning tent. I saw people helplessly running out of the burning building. I opened my eyes quickly. If this was praying, I didn't want it.

"This is hard."

"When you pray for others, it is an act of love and empathy. Sometimes we don't know who it is we carry with us in our hearts."

"What if they can't forgive me?" I asked. "What if ... I don't want to forgive them?" I thought of my mom again.

"Forgiving is one of the hardest things to do. But there is light even in the darkness."

We sat in an easy silence together for some time, staring into the fire as the logs were slowly reduced to hot coals.

"Well, I better get in before I catch a chill," Alice said. "Alfred's probably wondering where I am. I'll see you tomorrow bright and early."

I felt bad that I had forgotten to put another log on for her.

"Goodnight," I said as I watched her make her way back to the lodge by the light of the moon.

I sat up alone by the dying fire until I was barely able to wiggle my toes from the cold.

～

The next morning a voice called out, "We're all going down to the sauna, wanna come?" It was the girl who had a black pirate patch on her eye to hide her hollow eye socket. She hadn't wanted anyone to know what happened to her, and I wouldn't have asked, but she eventually confided to the group of us in our sharing circle that she was a professional car thief who, after one too many break-and-enters, got caught by the wrong person and was clubbed in the eye with a metal pipe.

"Sure, I guess." I hadn't even known there was a sauna until she mentioned it.

It was hidden deep in the bush on a trail where the trees looked like they could reach out and grab you.

The sauna was made of shipped-in, treated cedar. It had a pile of stones in the corner next to some benches inside. It was the type of sauna you'd see in a public swimming pool, made to please tourists with the need to escape to a more rustic luxury. The girl with the eye patch, Pam, stood by the hot rocks and every so often poured lake water over them, drawn from a metal bowl with a carved wooden spoon. When the room filled with steam and became unbearably hot, we all ran outside and jumped into the snowbank to cool off until we got too cold and had to warm up again inside.

It was invigorating.

I went every day after that. Sometimes George would join us and bring his drum, and we'd all sit in the darkness of the sauna under the northern lights and listen to him sing his sad warrior cries. The songs never failed to bring a lump to my throat.

~

Towards the end of our stay out at Alice's bush camp, George managed to track down the sneaky wolverine that kept coming too close to camp.

"Who wants to come check the traps with me?" he asked.

I volunteered. I had finished my chores early and was looking for something to do.

We walked a good ways and I had to peel some layers off to keep up. If he had warned me he was a speed walker I might have changed my mind about going with him.

When we reached the spot where George set his trap, he held his arm up to keep me back.

"Got 'em," he whispered with a victorious smile.

"How do you know?" I asked. I didn't see any sign of the wolverine or smell it for that matter.

"The trees. They're cleared out." He pointed in front of us. "Stay behind me."

He walked slowly into the opening in the birch trees and I followed cautiously. There it was, wrangled and snarling, its leg caught in the lasso of wire George rigged up. When George said the word trap, I'd pictured one of those old rusty metal traps with teeth but this one was more humane. When the wolverine saw us, it shot into action and spun around in a craze, so diabolical that I couldn't keep my eyes on it. It made sense why the trees around it were cleared out. Chips of wood and broken branches dusted the snow as far as the animal could reach as it tried to free itself, hitting and clawing at the trees.

Without warning, George took a shot and I jumped.

"Gotta put it out of its misery," he said.

He waited until the animal stopped moving to go near it. I stayed back, afraid. I could have sworn I saw it open its eyes for a moment, as if it were faking its own death, but if I told George, he'd probably think I was seeing things.

I should have though, because when George knelt down to

remove the wire around the wolverine's back leg, the animal came back to life, more violent than before. It moved with such chaos that George fell backwards and had to back away on the palms of his hands. Thankfully he hadn't removed the trap from the animal's back leg or I'm afraid we'd both be dead. George grabbed for his gun and shot at the vicious animal again until he was sure it was dead.

You better believe that the following winter, George sported the most jaw-dropping wolverine mitts anyone had ever seen, made by none other than Auntie Alice.

TEN

The fire season was over, but that didn't mean there were no more fires to fight. Wood stove fires were pretty common, even though only a small population of the community still had one after the government came in and replaced them with electric furnaces, rendering most of the community completely dependent on the power corporation to keep them warm.

There was the guy who burned his house down because the band wouldn't help fix it up after numerous maintenance requests. He thought he'd claim it as an accident and get the insurance but everyone knew it was him.

Then there were the unexplained fires. They started small. A burning rag doused in gasoline left to burn on the side of the road. Next, abandoned cars were set on fire.

My chest felt heavy. This looked like my work.

Then, one of the old wooden bridges, no longer serving a purpose due to the drought, burned to the ground, and that's when I knew something wasn't quite right. The crew had to battle the large fire in the dead of winter. I could tell by the box of matches strewn on the ground that it was hasty and poorly thought out. This wasn't just someone carelessly tossing a cigarette out the car window.

A pyro was on the loose.

"When I find out who's starting these fires, boy ..." Mav said angrily to Cayenne over at the band office. I happened to be in earshot as I helped make lunch for the Elders.

"Another one?" Cayenne asked.

"Last night, old man Noel's house went up in flames in the middle of the night. Thankfully no one was in there," Sup told her.

"That house was over a hundred years old. It was a piece of history," Cayenne said sadly. "This is getting out of hand. What can we do?"

"Catch 'em while they're in the act. Set up a night patrol if we have to." Mav was worked up.

"It's only one person," I said, and everyone turned to me.

"What?" Mav asked.

"It's only a kid."

"Why do you think that?" Sup asked curiously.

I knew I shouldn't have said anything but now it was too late. I had to explain. I took a deep breath. "Whoever's doing it does the same thing every time. They go through an entire box of matches before they're able to get one lit."

"And?" Mav didn't quite catch on to what I was getting at.

"They have a hard time striking a match." I'd gone over the areas with Sup and saw the devastation as we tried to piece together the forensics. We both found the matches at the bridge and at the old house but couldn't piece together the clues. I was up all night trying to wrap my mind around the evidence until it hit me that it had to have been someone who wasn't used to using matches.

"So you really think it's a kid?" Sup said.

"It's definitely a kid."

"Thanks, Nyla. You make a good point, but if he's still out there he'll do it again. The worst part is, it's gotta be one of the kids from the reserve," said Cayenne.

"If only the snow would stay on the ground long enough, we'd track him down no problem," Mav said.

"Whoever's doing this is probably hurting and needs some sort of release." I surprised myself with such wisdom. If only I could grant myself that type of understanding.

"That makes sense. There's a few kids we know of that are struggling right now. We try our best to help them, but some don't want our help. You know who I'm talking about, eh Mav?" Sup asked.

"I know exactly who you're talking about," Mav said seriously.

"They just lost their mother not too long ago, didn't they?" Sup asked.

"Yes, it's so unfortunate. I don't know what they're going to do now without her," Cayenne said sadly. "Should we bring the police into this? I mean this is a criminal investigation now, isn't it? This is what? The fourth suspicious fire now? And it doesn't look like whoever's doing it is going to stop anytime soon," Cayenne said with genuine concern.

"Nah. The police won't do anything anyway. They'll just get in the way. I'll go over to Brutus's place and have a talk," Mav said.

"Okay but be careful. Don't make any accusations." Cayenne sounded worried. She turned to me. "Thanks for your help, Nyla. Maybe you should go along with Mav. Mav, what do you think?"

"Yeah, why not. I might need a witness," he joked.

"Just to warn you, Brutus is ... well, he's quite the brute," Mav said just as we pulled up to Brutus's house, which at first I had mistaken for a scrap metal yard. The dilapidated house was surrounded by broken down skidoos, mismatched skis sticking out of an old barrel, bike rims, tire rims, copper wire, and an old camper van with the windows blown out. The rest of the yard was flattened by tire tracks and a littered driveway.

The house was missing the door to the porch, and you could see a gap in the floor of the unfinished addition. It had been built by someone with good intentions who lacked carpentry skills, using the wrong materials to patch things up. At the front step, empty beer cans, some garbage and a few bikes without kickstands had been thrown onto the ground as if someone jumped off mid-ride.

"This is it. What an eyesore," Mav said as he turned off his loud truck.

I wasn't one to judge. At least whoever lived inside had a roof over their head.

A few small kids peeked through the ripped curtain behind a cracked window and quickly hid when our eyes caught. An older girl stepped out onto the front porch with a baby in her arms and what looked to be another one on the way. She rested one of the child's legs on her protruding belly.

"That's Scarlett, Brutus's oldest. It's a bunch of kids taking care of kids now with their mother gone. Wait here, I guess." Mav got out of the truck.

"Hey Scarlett, is your dad around?"

"What do you want?" Her voice sounded kind but her face had "go away" written all over it.

"There's a kid starting fires back on the reserve, just wanna ask him if he knows anything about it, that's all," Mav said.

"We don't know about any fires," she said defensively.

Just then a boy not much taller than Scarlett walked out of the house twirling a pocket-knife in his hand. His pants didn't fit him; they were too small and exposed a pair of unmatched socks.

"What's up, Mav?" The way the boy said Mav's name was almost taunting, testing.

"Hello, Xavier."

"What do you want, man?"

"Do you know anything about the fire over at old man Noel's house?"

"Why you asking me?" Xavier said, jumping off the porch and making his way closer to Mav.

"Just want to know if you've seen anything that's all. Is your dad around?" Mav tried to sound relaxed.

"Why you wanna talk to my dad?" Xavier scowled.

"He's not home right now," Scarlett said assertively, backing up her brother.

"Who's that?" Xavier asked, pointing the knife in my direction.

"That's Nyla. She's on our fire crew," Mav said. When they all looked over at me I didn't know what to do. Should I introduce myself? Should I get out of the vehicle? I thought better of it and just waved awkwardly. No one waved back.

"Just let your dad know we came by," Mav said as he turned and walked back to the truck.

"Yah, that's right, get off our property!" Xavier hollered as Mav jumped into the truck and let out a quick exhale of relief.

"Shut up," Scarlett scolded her little brother, and they walked back into the house.

Before Mav could pull away, a large man walked out onto the uneven porch. If he were an animal, he would have been a bear no doubt. His large, round belly stuck out under his white tank. His face was weathered and gruff.

"What the commotion out here?" he grumbled, looking like he just woke up out of hibernation, scratching his underbelly. He looked like a perfect candidate for a massive heart attack as he hacked up half a lung and spit a wad of phlegm off the porch.

"Brutus. How are ya?" Mav said calmly, stepping cautiously back out of the truck but using the door as a body shield and talking through the open window.

"What the hell do you want?" Brutus said, now rubbing at his eye as his vision adjusted to the light outside.

"Well, there's been a few fires — "

"Ain't none of these kids done it," Brutus said, giving the side eye to Xavier. "You better get on out of here. Don't you know you're on private property? This ain't the reserve, Maverick."

Brutus didn't have to say it twice. "Okay, well, you have a good rest of the day," Mav said and he tipped his baseball cap like a cowboy and reversed out.

I could see Brutus from the rearview mirror already yelling at Xavier and hitting him hard on the back of his head as he walked back into the house. For a moment our eyes met; he was looking at me in fear as we drove away, and in that moment, I knew he didn't do it.

"It's not Xavier. He's not starting the fires."

"How do you know?"

"I just know. He's too innocent. He just acts tough. He has to."

"Well, we can't do much anyway until we have proof. Brutus is the biggest criminal around. He's been up to no good for years. He's one of our band members but refuses to have anything to do with the community."

"How many kids does he have?"

"I stopped counting. Nine, maybe ten? I can't imagine having that many kids," Mav continued.

At least they had each other, I thought.

"We're not gonna get anywhere with Brutus if it's one of his lot," Mav told Cayenne back at the band office as he poured a cup of cold coffee into a styrofoam cup, followed with a generous amount of sugar.

"I figured as much." Cayenne didn't look up from her computer. She was busy at work while a few of the regular visitors sat at some of the public-use computers, playing solitaire and pretending not to listen.

"We'll just have to catch whoever's doing it in the act, I guess," Mav said.

"How are we going to do that?" asked Cayenne. She was never about acting like she knew everything under the sun just because she was voted in as Chief. To her, "a leader is someone who seeks the advice of others."

"We just wait, I guess, and keep a close eye out, let everyone know to report anything suspicious," said Mav.

Cayenne asked a few of the locals to keep an eye out for anything that looked out of the ordinary and do some nightly rounds in the community. The two security patrols hired were big guys. Although not very fast on their feet, if they caught you there was no getting away, and it wasn't long before they caught the arsonist.

Who I thought was Brutus's youngest daughter was caught in the middle of the night pouring gas on another abandoned house down the road from the cemetery, the last house bordering the reserve. She stole the gas can from one of the guards doing rounds in the community.

I heard the whole story back at the band office the next day as I sat in the next room and listened to them talk in a whisper.

"They caught her red-handed," Mav said. "I can't believe it."

"Are you sure she did it?" Cayenne asked, wanting it to be anyone else but her.

"She was sneaking around Giroux's property. He followed her on foot and found her pouring gas around the perimeter of the old empty house. Chased her down thinking it was Xavier. She ran and hid in Mary Jane's yard and stashed the jerry can under the deck."

"I just can't imagine Nayiihtła doing something like this. She's so quiet and polite. So, what do we do now?" Cayenne asked.

"Do we turn her in?" Mav asked, clearly at a loss of what to do.

"Let me talk to Alice and the other Elders to see what they think first. This is a cry for help."

When Brutus died, he didn't go out in a blaze of glory like his lifestyle would have led one to expect. Instead, his ailing health slowly brought him to his end. He was overweight, red in the face and always huffing and puffing, out breath and full of anger. Probably inevitable, he suffered a major heart attack. Some said it was heartbreak from the loss of his children's mother.

With Brutus gone, the kids were placed in a foster home that had enough room to fit them all without having to separate them.

Although he was not well liked, the entire community showed up for Brutus's funeral. The kids were brought back to the reserve to attend their father's funeral and sat in the back corner by the wash-rooms. Dressed in brand new clothes paid for by social services. They watched as people ate and visited with one another, no one seeming to care that their dad's dead body was lying in a coffin in the corner of the room and that it may have been traumatizing for them.

Cayenne talked to Alice and the Elders council about what to do about Nayiihtła. Unbeknownst to me, they came to the conclusion that since both Nayiihtła and I had a similar affinity to fire, it would be good for her to stay with me while she completed her community sentence.

I was called into Cayenne's office to speak with the Elders council once they came to an agreement on what needed to be done. Nayiihtła was sitting in the corner of the hallway on an empty chair, waiting for the verdict alone in the dark. I guessed that she couldn't have been more than ten. She didn't bother to look up at me as I passed by.

Cayenne and Alice sat in the prayer room at a round table painted like a drum. On the floor there was a large medicine wheel rug. The room was full of posters that warned about the use of drugs and alcohol. It was where the band held their weekly sewing circles and AA meetings.

"And what if I can't do it alone?"

"You won't be alone. We will help too," Alice had said reassuringly.

It took some coaxing, but I eventually agreed reluctantly. Nayiihtła didn't have any belongings with her other than what she carried her on her back when she moved into the camper with me. The camper had a second bedroom on the other end with a bunk bed in it. The small bedroom was barely big enough to fit anyone lying down, so it was a good thing she wasn't tall, or her feet would hang out the door.

"Do you drink coffee?" I asked her when she stepped out of the camper in the late morning after the first night. Not quite the early bird, I got myself up not long before her and sat outside by the fire waiting for the water in the old tin kettle to percolate from where it sat, crooked atop a metal grate that formed a bridge between two rocks.

"I'm a kid, I don't drink coffee."

"I see. How about tea?"

"So how long do I gotta stay here with you anyway?"

"Your guess is as good as mine."

She gave me a snarly look.

"Listen, I'm sorry this is happening to you. I can't imagine how hard it must be to lose your parents."

"Why'd they put me with *you* anyway?" She was blunt and to the point.

"I guess it's 'cause I was once like you," I said slowly.

"Oh yeah? Like how?"

"I set fires too."

"Who said I started those fires? Maybe it was an accident." She was still not owning up to her actions.

"Listen, I get it. I'm just as confused as you are with this whole situation. I'm just doing what was asked of me."

"Well I don't need anyone to take care of me. I'm going for a walk. I'll be back later."

"Umm, all right." I thought of what a parent would say. "Just don't be too late?"

"Yeah, whatever," she clapped back.

But she didn't come back. In fact, she didn't come back at all that night. I hoped she wouldn't be foolish enough to start another fire. She was on her last chance. I waited up for her and paced the trailer, not knowing what to do. Was it my responsibility to keep an eye on her at all times? This was exactly why I was reluctant to look after her. I could barely look after myself, let alone an out-of-control kid. I woke before the sun came up and decided to take it upon myself to try to track her down.

When I couldn't find her, I went to tell Cayenne that Nayiihtła ran away, and that's when I found out she'd been in an accident. No one was home but there was a note on the door to Mav which I could barely understand other than being able to sound out the familiar words hospital and accident.

Turns out she stole a car down the road from Cayenne's house and smashed it into the neighbour's parked car. The owner went running after her on foot, and as she sped off she nearly ran him over.

"I didn't see him standing there. He was in the middle of the road," Nayiihtła said in her defence when Cayenne asked what had happened. Cayenne stood at her hospital bedside while I sat in the corner of the room, not knowing how to be on the other side of a crisis.

"I couldn't stop; it was too slippery. The windows were fogged."

"You're lucky you didn't hit him. You would have killed him," Mav scolded from the other side of the hospital bed.

Nayiihtła rolled her eyes at both of them and continued to struggle to get free, but she was strapped to the bed with a thick belt that had a lock over her waist.

"It's for your own protection." The way Cayenne said it in such an empathetic way made it known that she didn't think it was right that Nayiihtła was being held down against her will.

"You're lucky to be alive," Cayenne added. "The car's a write-off now. Why? What'd you do it for anyways?" Mav asked.

"You're not my parents."

Just then the doctor walked in.

He walked up to Nayiihtła and looked into her pupils with a flashlight. "She'll need to stay here a few more days. We need to assess her."

"Assess me?" Nayiihtła asked.

"We just want to make sure you're getting the right care is all. We know you've been through a lot," the doctor said as he looked to Mav and Cayenne. "Can I have a word with you two outside?"

I followed them out into the hallway, looking back at Nayiihtła who had given up squirming and stared out the window blankly.

"What's with the waistband? She's not an animal," Cayenne cried.

"She tried to leave after being admitted, and we had to call the guards to stop her for her own good. She put up a fight and nearly broke one of the guard's arms. We have to keep her and our staff safe. It's hospital policy."

"She's probably scared. She's been through a lot." Cayenne kept advocating for Nayiìhtła.

"Well, that's precisely why I wanted to have a word with you. Have you ever known Nayiìhtła to be suicidal?"

"You think she crashed on purpose?" asked Cayenne.

"It's possible. There are facilities down south that can help her with whatever it is she is going through."

"What if she doesn't want to go down south?" I asked.

The doctor ignored me and snapped his clipboard shut.

"It's possible that she tried taking her own life last night and could have killed someone and herself. We must take incidents like this very seriously."

Mav nodded in agreement. "Whatever needs to be done to help her, I guess."

Cayenne disagreed with her brother and the doctor. "How is that going to help her? I've seen other kids get sent down south, only for them never to return home. I've heard horrible stories about what's happened to them."

I went back into the room to let them hash it out and sat by Nayiìhtła's side for a bit even though her face said "go away." I stayed even after Mav and Cayenne left to go back home.

"You don't have to be here you know," she said after a few hours of us sitting in silence as the TV played cheap game shows flooded with commercials.

"I wasn't sure if you wanted company or not," I said. "I can come back again tomorrow?"

"Do you know when they're gonna let me out of here?"

"Maybe in a few days. I'm not sure." I didn't want to be the one to tell her she might be in there a lot longer or even sent down south to a different hospital.

"Why a few days? I feel fine. I'm not even hurt."

"They just want to make sure you're okay. You've been through a lot."

"Why does everyone keep saying that?"

I was quiet then. I could see she'd been masking her tears with anger. She must have felt safe enough with me because she started crying like a child.

I didn't know what to do, if I should stay or go. If I should hug her as she lay there alone on the hospital bed or let her be. So, I just sat there, trying not to look in her direction too much, hoping that maybe in some small way I was offering comfort just by being by her side.

She put her arm up over her eyes to hide her tears as she cried, and it was then that I noticed them. The burn marks up and down her arms. Cigarette burns. Round red dots lined along the back of her forearm.

The scars of the past could not be fixed by any doctor or any tests they might run on her.

Suddenly embarrassed, she wiped her tears and immediately stopped crying. "You can go now," she said coldly.

After a week of back and forth between Cayenne and the doctors, the hospital reluctantly agreed to release Nayiihtła back into my care with the promise that Cayenne would check in on her every day.

I waited by the elevators for Nayiihtła to be released. When she walked out of the hospital ward she was still wearing her blue gown with her jacket overtop without her arms in it. Her bloodied clothes from the car accident were in a plastic bag. She had a prescription for some strong anti-depressants, sleeping pills, and something to help quiet the voices in her head that she had confessed to hearing from time to time. Cayenne didn't think it was necessary for the doctor to put her on so many medications. She strongly believed that being outside on the land was the best remedy, but the doctors didn't see it that way no matter how much she tried to argue her point.

Back at the camper, I lit a fire and sat outside while Nayiihtła went inside and changed her clothes.

"I bet you're glad to be out of there." I poured her some tea and she hesitantly sat by the fire on a wobbly log.

"It felt like jail."

"I know the feeling."

"Anything's better than that place."

"Even this old run-down camper?" I tried to make light of things.

"I guess, yeah."

"It's not that bad once you get used to it, minus the outhouse. I don't think I could ever get used to that," I said trying to make her laugh and getting a hint of a smile.

"You know, Elder Alice took me to a place out across the lake that people go to for healing. Maybe we can ask her to take us there when the weather gets warmer? I don't know about you, but I could sure use a getaway."

~

ELEVEN

"The lake looks like a giant pterodactyl."

"Wow. It does." I turned my head sideways to see what Nayiihtła was seeing on the map. We had become friends having to live in such close quarters. We tolerated one another and over time got used to each other's company, which could have just as easily gone the opposite way as well.

It was finally summer and our long-awaited getaway — or "staycation" as Nayiihtła called it, since it wasn't like we were going to a tropical destination — was about to commence. We were headed out to the great and mysterious waterfall that Alice had only spoken about briefly, but I suspected it was the same waterfall she told me about when she took me to the Thousand Islands.

The fire season hadn't yet begun and was forecasted to be off to a slow start because it had been an exceptionally rainy spring.

"We'll go through this narrow channel here, Babàcho's Channel," said Cayenne.

"Why's it called that?" Nayiihtła asked.

"It's where an old lake creature named Babàcho lives under the water. Babàcho means grandfather."

"We lost a lot of relatives in this area who didn't know what they were doing out on the water. Babàcho watches out for us," said Sizeh.

"How long does it take to get to the waterfall?" I asked.

"Half a day if the weather's good," replied Alice. "But we're in no rush. We'll take our time and stop along the way. We're going to stop at a sand bar and beaver dam but first, we must go to the Thousand

Islands." Alice looked directly at me. "You have some unfinished business there."

I nodded and took in a deep, satisfying breath. I was ready.

The boat was big enough to sleep the few of us who went: me, Nayiìhtła, Cayenne, Alice and Sizeh. It had a small kitchen and two sleeping nooks; the one that was hidden underneath the stairs was where Nayiìhtła and I would sleep. Sizeh would sleep up top under the stars and watch out for us. The cabin was so small we had to crawl low to the ground to get in and out. I stayed on the deck under the stars listening to Alice tell stories until I was too tired to stay awake and could be easily lulled to sleep by the gentle waves rocking the boat.

Being that it was rainier than usual that spring, I was hopeful that the pool was full. Not only for myself, but for Nayiìhtła too. We all helped set up camp when we arrived at the island, as we would be staying there for the night before heading out through Babàcho's Channel on our way towards the great waterfall.

"Ready?" Alice asked after she had a light snack.

"Yes." I said, and we walked back to the hole in the rock that had been left uncovered since I'd last been there.

"It took many, many rains to fill this pool. It froze over and thawed again," Alice said as I looked down and saw my own reflection in the still water. The pool was filled to the brim, spilling over onto the ground.

Alice had brought a grease screen, which she used to scoop out the dead bugs and leaves.

"Do you remember what to do?" she asked.

"I think so."

"Come back here tonight and bathe under the light of the moon. They're both full."

Back at our tent, Nayiìhtła and I played rock-paper-scissors to see who would go in first.

I lost.

I grabbed a towel and took the short hike to the other side of the small island. I knelt beside the pool and looked up at the moon.

Was I supposed to go in fully clothed? I forgot to ask. Probably not. I looked around to make sure no one was looking and undressed quickly. I tested the water with my hands first. It was a perfect temperature. I lowered myself slowly and splashed my face first and then cupped the water to wet my hair.

How long was I supposed to stay in? According to Alice, something miraculous was supposed to occur. But when? I waited for something to happen, but nothing did. I stayed in until my fingers pruned. Just before getting out, I plugged my nose and sunk to the bottom, where I held my breath for as long as I could.

"Your turn," I said to Nayiihtła when I got back to our shared tent. But there was no response.

"Nayiihtła?"

Nothing.

"Where'd she go?" I asked myself out loud.

Maybe she already went to the pool, but she would have had to pass me on the trail. She probably went to go get a snack from one of the containers under the tarp by the fire pit, I thought. I didn't bother checking. We were on a small enough island that she couldn't have gone far. Besides, it wasn't like she was a small child who needed to be tended to constantly. I was tired from the day and in such an extremely relaxed state from the pool that once I put my head down to rest, I was out instantly.

I slept peacefully through the night. The next morning Nayiihtła was still nowhere to be seen. It was only then that I began to really worry. I walked to the communal fire where Sizeh was already up cooking a can of beans for breakfast on the open flame.

"Good morning, Sizeh, have you seen —"

Just then I saw a glimpse of the back of Nayiihtła's head. She was standing on the other side of the blue tarp.

Sizeh just stood there waiting for me to finish my sentence.

"Oh, it's okay. Found her," I said, and he just looked at me, bemused.

"You're up early. How was the water?" I asked as I walked over to her. She was standing in the sunlight picking the yellow berries off the branches.

"I felt like I was floating in outer space in an endless abyss," she said poetically — or sarcastically — I couldn't tell the difference with her sometimes.

"Wow, okay. That's a lot more than what I felt."

"Oh? That's too bad," she said, not really seeming to care.

"It was invigorating, don't get me wrong, but I also felt like it took a lot out of me. I guess healing doesn't just happen overnight."

The beach in Coppertown was artificial, but this one was natural. Cayenne wasn't joking when she said it looked like a tropical paradise. The sand was as white as the snow. It looked like a postcard.

When we pulled up on shore, Sizeh had to tie the boat to a large boulder atop the gradual slope of sand that slowly poured into the lake. The wind swept the delicate silt up into the air and into the water, where it dissolved like sugar. The sand mound was so high off the ground it looked like it had been dumped there by a giant child playing in a sandbox. In the distance, the landscape was similar to the rest of the North, jagged skinny trees and rock that made the white sand beach an anomaly, out of place from everything around it.

"It's not quicksand," Nayiihtła laughed at me when I took a long pause before getting out of the boat, even though I was only stopping to admire a landscape I had never seen before.

She had taken to lightheartedly teasing me at every chance she got, but I didn't mind. At least it made her happy.

We walked along the beach where leaves jutted out at our feet. "What kind of grass is this?" I asked.

"They're trees," Alice said.

"Trees?" Nayiihtła asked curiously.

"We're standing on the top of birch trees," Cayenne said.

"Eventually all this sand will pour out into the lake," said Alice.

"Industry wants to take it out of here by barge, but we keep saying no. We don't ever benefit from what they do when they take from our lands," Cayenne said.

"What do they want it for?" I asked.

"They want to use it to make those new phones. This is the finest sand in the world; that's why they want to get their hands on it so bad," said Cayenne, who was the one constantly hounded by industry for consultation.

I crouched down and let a handful of the translucent beads slip through my fingers.

"It looks like glass," Nayiihtła commented.

We explored a bit, and I found a good walking stick, which Nayiihtła said made me look like a sheep herder from way back in biblical times. A large-looking boulder sat in the centre of the highest point of sand and Nayiihtła and I took turns trying to climb onto it. It was one giant cluster of rocks stuck together, and pieces of it fell off in my hand when I tried to get a good grip. I gave up trying to climb it and let Nayiihtła step on my hands to get up.

"What's it like up there?" I asked.

"I can see forever!" she said happily. She jumped down and landed on the soft sand. "Look." She pointed at a rock in the perfect shape of a heart and picked it up.

"Hey, it's a heart," I said, impressed.

"Do you want it?"

"Finders keepers." She needed it more than I did, I thought.

"We'll share it," she said and put it in her pocket.

Alice met us at the boulder. "We better get going, we've got a long trip ahead of us."

Back at the boat I untied the ropes and helped Cayenne push off from shore while Sizeh lowered the engines into the water.

"Look," I said loudly, pointing to a ribbon of smoke in the distance on a small island that looked no bigger than our boat.

"Is it a forest fire?" Nayiihtła asked.

"There's a spot on that island that burns every so often to remind us that our Ancestors are with us," said Cayenne.

"The scientists tried to tell us we are wrong. What did they call it? A mirror?" Alice couldn't remember the word.

"A mirage." Cayenne was good at guessing the words when Alice couldn't remember them.

"Yes, a mirage, but we know better. It's more than that."

When we got closer to the smoke, it began to disappear, but as we made our way towards Babàcho's Channel, I couldn't help but look back to see the smoke rising in a straight line all the way up into the sky. Was that what caught the trees on fire when I was alone on the island? The Ancestors? I wanted to ask but decided to save it for another time. I had so many questions but was starting to learn that the answers would come to me when the time was right.

We made it through Babàcho's Channel without a hitch, but I could see how it could pose trouble for an inexperienced boater. It was a sharp turn into a narrow passage, and if missed, the wind could sweep a boat out to the middle of the lake, where a series of "whirlpools waited to capsize anything in their wake," Sizeh warned in his language and Cayenne translated for us. Cayenne added, "This is where we sometimes see Babàcho. He's got eyes as big and as far apart as two headlights on a rig," said Cayenne, as Sizeh steered us away from the churning water.

"And why are they only telling us this now?" Nayiihtła whispered as she huddled close to me in fear.

"They say he travels the bottom of the lake in underground tunnels. He's prehistoric," said Cayenne.

"No one knows how deep the lake is," Alice said.

I found it intriguing to think that there could be something living in the water. I wasn't afraid but would have probably changed my mind if it resembled a giant jackfish.

The waves subsided once we were through the rough channel.

"There they are. The underwater mountains." Cayenne pointed to a large wall of solid rock that looked like a small city rising out of the middle of the lake in front of us.

"That's where were going?" I asked, wide-eyed.

"Yes. We're gonna climb it," Alice said with ease.

"Climb?" Nayiíhtła cried.

Alice saw my eyes go wide. "Don't worry, it's not that hard."

When we got nearer, Sizeh pulled right up to the rock face, and the boat floated so close to the massive wall that we could reach out and touch the marbled granite. Small trees and bird's nests balanced on miniscule ledges directly above us. How anything could grow there was beyond me. The rock slabs piled on top of each other, forming thick columns. Within small holes in the rock, I could see narrow caves, a perfect location for a bat sanctuary.

"Some people pay a lot of money to have their kitchen counters made out of this stuff," Cayenne said, marvelling at the marble. "I'm always speechless when I come out here."

"We are at the peak of a large mountain that falls thousands of feet below us," Alice said.

I wasn't so much worried about what was below us but rather what was above us. "How are we gonna get up there?" I asked.

"Rope." Alice grabbed long coils of blue rope from under one of the seats with carabiners attached. "There's a spot just around the corner that's a bit easier to climb. It's a more gradual slope." As if it would make us feel better, she added, "I'll go first."

Being an Elder didn't stop Alice from keeping active. When she wasn't climbing mountains, she was wringing out hides with her bare hands or canoeing against the waves. Her life had been full of hard work on the land and water, which kept her nimble and strong.

"Coming back down is the hard part," she yelled from above when she reached the top without dropping a sweat.

"C'mon, Nyla, your turn." Cayenne helped me into my harness and tugged hard on the rope to make sure it was secure.

"Okay, she's ready," Cayenne yelled up to Alice.

Was I?

Cayenne pulled on one end of the rope while Alice pulled the other end from the top so I climbed with support. As I lifted into the air, I grabbed onto the rope with the leather mitts Alice gave me and planted both feet on the rock to prevent myself from crashing into it. But when a few pebbles came loose and dropped onto the front deck of the boat below, I yelled, "I'm scared!"

"Don't look down. Remember, you jumped out of a helicopter. You got this," Cayenne encouraged.

Right. Except this time I wasn't saving anyone except myself.

"Now what?" I asked Alice when I met her at the top after a few more encouraging words from Cayenne.

"We jump," Alice smiled.

I nearly choked on air. "You're joking, right?" I couldn't believe what I was hearing.

"I made it!" Nayiihtła said as she pulled herself up and over the ledge on her stomach. "That was intense."

"I don't think I can do it," I said to Alice.

"Do what?" Nayiihtła asked.

"Well, it is the fastest way down," Alice said, stating the obvious.

"She wants us to jump?" Nayiihtła hollered.

"Are you jumping?" I asked Alice in a small voice.

"No. There's an emergency elevator on the other side. I'll be taking that," she teased. "I'm going to rappel down. I've done this jump many times when I was younger, but it's too much for me now.

I'll see you at the bottom." With that she rigged herself back up into the harness.

"So this is one of the healing pools?" I asked, just wanting to be sure. For some reason I thought they all would be a hole in the rock, just in a different place.

"Yes, one of them." Alice said as she gave the signal to Cayenne to pull the rope.

I looked over at Nayiihtła, who was pacing back and forth from the edge and biting her nails. "I don't think I can do this. Let's just rappel down." Nayiihtła watched Alice hop and run down the side of the rock with only one hand holding the rope. "I mean if she can do it, we can do it too."

"Right." I said, but something in me didn't want to take the easy way. "But if I can jump then so can you. Let's jump together."

"Like on the count of three?" She asked.

"Yeah."

"I don't know."

"C'mon, it's okay. It's not that far down. Just plug your nose."

"Okay …" She reached for my hand, still unsure.

We stood at the very edge.

"Ready?" I asked.

She looked at me and shook her head.

"One, two — " I counted slowly.

"Wait." She let go of my hand and backed away. "Don't we have to say a prayer or something?"

"Oh, yeah."

"Like, pray we don't die?" She laughed in fear.

I laughed. My heart was beating so fast with adrenaline that I closed my eyes and took a moment.

"Think of the ones you love, the ones that need forgiveness and the ones you hope will forgive you," I said, like Alice taught me.

When the long moment of silence was over, I peeked over at Nayiihtła. "Ready?"

She took a deep breath and nodded slightly.

"Three … two — "

"Wait. It's supposed to be one … two … three."

I jumped when she said three.

I hit the water feet first like an arrow piercing through the heart and everything went dark. For a split second I saw a woman who looked like me, a much older version with a small, smiling child holding her hand. The baby's laugh was the most joyful sound I ever heard, but it was just as quickly replaced by the sound of water rushing into my ears and forcing me back into the present. I wrestled through the current that circled me, almost pulling me under until I fought against it and made it to the surface. Sizeh leaned over the back of the boat and reached out his hand to help me up onto the ladder.

"You did it!" Alice and Cayenne cheered.

I sat on the back of the boat out of breath, trying to understand what I had witnessed.

I looked up to see Nayiihtła looking apologetic. She shrugged her shoulders. "I'm sorry!" she mouthed from above. She changed her mind at the last moment; she would have to rappel down. Alice handed me a towel and rubbed my back to help control my shaking body.

"Are you mad at me?" Nayiihtła asked on the ride to our next stop.

I shook my head and smiled. "No."

Maybe I had to go it alone for my own personal healing journey. She had her own journey, and maybe she just wasn't ready.

We stopped in a sheltered inlet for lunch. The shoreline was shaped like a crescent moon and the beach was covered with thousands of sharp shards of shale that made a satisfying crunching sound as we walked across them. I picked two pieces and clinked them together. They broke in my hands, so delicate and fine yet so sharp they could slice like a knife.

That evening we sat around the campfire before we moved back to the boat for the night, and Alice and Cayenne told the story of the waterfall and why it was so sacred.

"There was a woman who was left behind long ago by her community," Cayenne started.

Alice continued, "There was a great famine and the community decided to move in search of food. She was too old and sick to go on the journey with them, so she offered to stay behind until the end of time on one condition: whoever came back to visit her would come in search of healing and bring her a gift from the heart."

"So that is what we do. We visit when we are in need of healing medicine and we share with her what is in our hearts," Cayenne said.

"And in turn she gives us strength," Alice said, matter-of-factly. "But first, we have to cross the giant tsà dam."

"What is that?" I asked.

"Tsà means beaver. Long ago giant beavers roamed the North."

Nayiìhtła interrupted with a cheeky snicker. "Giant beavers? For real?"

I nudged her with my elbow.

Alice didn't pay any mind to Nayiìhtła's childish interruption. "Beavers are very family oriented. They live together in their lodge houses with many rooms for their offspring. One day when the giant tsà was out collecting wood, the white man came and killed his family for their fur. When he returned, they were gone. Now the giant tsà lives alone, hoping one day to be reunited with his family. He built a dam so strong that no one can break through it. If it ever does break, there will be a great flood. This is why we pay our respects to that area when we pass by. He is very bitter and does not like to be disturbed, but we must pass by the dam to get to the waterfall," Alice explained.

"For a long time, researchers scoffed at our stories about the giant beavers that roamed these areas for millennia, but now they've found proof we were right all along. The skeleton of some of their remains have been found," said Cayenne.

"Bigger than a sahcho," Sizeh added.

"Yes. They were once bigger than a large bear," Alice said.

"That dam's been there for hundreds of years, unbroken," Cayenne explained.

"How do we pay our respects?" I asked.

"With an offering," said Alice.

"Like feeding the fire?"

"Yes. We'll give you some tobacco to put down."

When we got to the dam the next day, the first thing we saw was a string of offerings dotted all along a solid wall that was made of sticks and branches.

"Here." Alice gave me a pinch of tobacco as I stood on the dam that formed a bridge across the narrow part of the lake, dividing it in half.

I placed the tobacco offering down and said my prayers to Creator the best I knew how. Just then a cool breeze blew through my hair, and I thought I heard the sound of something in the bushes not too far from where we stood.

I opened my eyes, "Did you hear that?" I asked.

"That's the tsà hard at work," Alice said.

"We can't see him, but sometimes we can hear him crashing through the trees," Cayenne said. "A severe forest fire swept through here a few years ago." Cayenne pointed at the swath of dead trees visible from where we stood. "The tsà has had to go further and further for lumber. If it keeps up this way with the fires, the dam might become too weak and break."

Nothing surprised me anymore, not even the hard-to-believe supernatural occurrences that seemed to always take place when I was with Alice. I knew not to question things but having to jump from where we stood was something I did question even if it was just a short distance to the water.

"Is this one of the pools?" I asked, scared to know the answer as I looked down into the waves that bashed into the wall as if to try and break through it.

"No!" Alice laughed lightheartedly. "Don't worry. You'll swim over there in the calmer waters," she pointed at the sheltered bay in the distance where we anchored the boat, "but for now that can wait. Let's eat first."

We had an exceptionally filling lunch of leftover bannock and jam, fresh fish that we caught earlier that morning and berries we collected at each stop. We all sat in the warm sun after lunch, talking mostly about the weather until it was almost too hot to bear.

"That water is looking more and more inviting," Cayenne said as she wiped the sweat off her forehead.

"Let's go then. What are we waiting for?" Alice said and walked into the water, wading up to her waist before diving under.

"The water's warm," she hollered as she did a back stroke further into the lake.

Nayiihtła had already retreated into the shade.

"You ready?" I asked her as I walked up to where she had taken up residence, leaning her back on a half-uprooted tree.

"I'm not feeling so well," she said and rubbed her stomach. "I think I ate too much. Go on without me. I'll be okay," she said.

"Okay. Hope you feel better," I said, not thinking too much of it. Already in my bathing suit, which I wore under my shorts and t-shirt, I grabbed my towel out of our shared bag.

The water was unbearably cold at first, but the longer I stayed in the easier it got. As Cayenne floated up beside me she said, "You can drink it you know. The minerals are good for you. It's not stagnant like that metal-tasting tap water we have back home on the reserve. The water's pure here."

She must have read my mind. The water was so crisp and clear it was too tempting not to drink it. I cupped my hands and took a big gulp and felt it instantly enliven every cell in my body.

"Wow, that is good!" I said. Even my heart felt aflutter.

"I think that's how Sizeh's managed to live so long. No one knows how old he actually is," she whispered. We laughed when we looked over and saw him floating on his back and spurting a fountain of water from his mouth.

The plan was to spend the night floating in the bay on the other side of the great tsà dam and leave early in the morning to reach the waterfall by noon. But I didn't get much sleep that night because I had to care for Nayiìhtła, who was so sick that she was in severe pain most of the night.

"I feel like I'm going to die."

"Maybe you ate too many berries," I said sympathetically.

"Can you just stay here beside me. I don't want to be alone right now. I'm scared."

"Of course. I'm not going anywhere." I let her head rest on my lap.

"What are you going to give to the Old Lady of the Falls tomorrow?" Nayiìhtła asked.

"I'm not sure." The truth was I was wracking my mind trying to figure out what I could offer.

"What about our heart?"

"Our heart?" I asked, puzzled.

"You know, the heart-shaped rock. The one we share."

"Oh yeah."

When she pulled it from her pocket and tried giving it to me, I noticed that her hand was trembling.

"But what are you going to give her?"

"I already have something in mind," she said.

I wanted to ask but maybe it was like a wish where you aren't supposed to tell anyone or it won't come true.

"Why don't you hold onto it for the night, so I don't forget," I said, and she fell asleep with the heart-shaped rock in her hand tucked close to her own heart while I stayed up counting the stars, watching the odd one shoot by.

The spectacular waterfall did not disappoint. It was not an exceptionally tall waterfall in the sense that it fell from a steep cliff, but more of a rushing river that curved and sloped gradually. The water was wrapped around ancient rock formations and burst between them with such force that it looked like it could have been released from the mighty tsà dam itself.

When we arrived, we saw a graveyard of crutches on the far side of the waterfall where Alice said people had abandoned them after being healed.

"Do you need more tobacco to put down?" Alice asked.

"Actually, I have something else I'd like to give," I said and showed her the heart-shaped rock that had fallen out of Nayiihtła's hand while she slept.

Alice held it and rubbed it with her thumb. She nodded and smiled in agreement. "This is just right. I'll leave you now. This is something you must do alone. Come back to the camp when you're done."

I watched the beautiful waterfall before me, trying to think of the right words to say. Waiting for the perfect time to make the offering. But there was no perfect time; there were no perfect words. I only needed to say what was in my heart. Then, just as I was about to drop the heart-shaped rock into the sacred pool below, Nayiihtła walked up behind me.

"Nyla." She said my name as if she had an announcement to make.

"Oh, I didn't hear you coming. Are you feeling better?"

"Sort of." She pointed to a thin veil of water that masked what looked to be a cave entrance behind it. "Do you think she's really in there?"

"Her spirit maybe." I wondered if she wanted to believe in the legends as much as I did.

"Do you think we could lower ourselves down the side to get a better look? I want to see if she's actually real," she said.

"I don't think it's a good idea," I said with a frown.

"Why not? We already climbed rocks much steeper than this."

"It's not that I'm scared. I just don't think it's a good idea."

"Don't you want to see her? Don't you want to see what the old lady looks like?"

"I don't need to see to believe."

After some persuasion, Nyla was somehow able to convince me to lower her down the side of the waterfall against my better judgement.

"Make sure you hold on tight and don't let go," I cautioned.

With only a rope that she must have taken from the boat tied under her arms, she was ready to be lowered down the rocks next to the waterfall.

"Wait," I said.

"What?"

"You sure you don't want to give her this yourself?" I showed her the rock she found.

"Keep it. Remember, it's yours." I could have sworn I saw tears in her eyes.

She slowly lowered herself down as I leaned back as far as possible and tried to control the amount of slack in the rope.

"I see something!" Nayiihtła suddenly yelled excitedly from beneath the ledge.

"What is it?" I yelled back.

"It's a light," she said curiously. I carefully stepped closer to the edge to peer over and saw her pointing to a dancing light shining through the misty water.

"It's probably just a reflection from the sun," I said, but she went to it like a moth to a flame.

"No!" I yelled to try and stop her, but she had already pushed off the rock and swung herself too far over, causing me to lose my balance.

I saw her slip into the waterfall, almost as if something pulled her in; at the same time I fell into the rushing water, its mist rising up into the atmosphere. I wanted to reach for her, to save her, but I couldn't even save myself. I was tossed around violently, tumbling inside of the enormous flood of water like a restless sleeper tangled in a sea of silk sheets. Time and space and light no longer existed.

I found myself suddenly somewhere else, walking across thin ice. My body grew colder. I stumbled upon an old shack and breathed fog on the window and wiped it away to look inside. I was so cold and needed shelter. A man looked at me in fear through the glass, as if I were a zombie. He didn't recognize me at first.

He said my name. My real name.

My face and hands were blue from the shock of cold water against my skin, and now I was outside in the cold of winter in the middle of nowhere. The pain from the cuts and scrapes and broken bones I endured from the fall were almost too much to bear. I fell to my knees.

The old man took me in and brought me to the oil lamp he had burning in the centre of his shack for warmth. For survival. He told me he'd been waiting for me to visit. I could hear him, but his mouth did not move. We spoke without words through the flames of the fire, somewhere between darkness and light. Then suddenly the flame diminished to a flicker and the water rushed into his shack, bursting the walls into oblivion.

"Nyla! Nyla!" Alice, Cayenne, and Sizeh came running down the slope as fast as they could when they heard my scream. Alice shook my shoulder when she reached me. "Nyla, are you okay?"

Water sputtered out of my mouth as they sat me up and patted my back.

"Where's Nayiihtła?" was all I could muster.

"Who?"

"Nayiihtła?" I said again in a panic.

"She must have hit her head," Cayenne said to Alice with concern.

"You're going to be okay, Nyla. Let's get you warm and dry." They helped me make my way to the warmth of a fire.

~

"I see now what has happened here," Alice said to me as I woke a second time to find myself tucked into a sleeping blanket in a canvas tent with the sound of the rushing waterfall outside. "Here, drink this." She gave me a cup of something warm and strong with the taste of spruce.

"Is Nayiıhtła okay?" I asked, suddenly remembering what happened.

"Nyla, you need to know something about Nayiıhtła."

"What do you mean? Where is she?" I stammered, worried she may not have survived. It would have been all my fault.

"The name Nayiıhtła means light, did you know that?" Alice said.

That didn't matter right now. I sat up and looked around the tent for Nayiıhtła, but it was just Alice and me.

"Is that what Nyla is short for? Nayiıhtła? Is that your name?" She treaded carefully, not wanting to alarm me more than I already was.

I saw a flash of the old man's face.

"Do you think someone else was with you at the waterfall? Someone with the name Nayiıhtła?" Alice whispered as she held my hand.

I trusted her. "Yes," I gulped. "Nayiıhtła was with me," I said, sounding more and more unsure.

"And who is Nayiıhtła to you?"

"She's … she's my friend. I was caring for her. You asked me to. Back at the sentencing circle."

"Nyla, the only sentencing circle you were at was the one we held for you when you stole the car," Alice said quietly and held my hand in both her hands.

"No. It can't be. I didn't steal a car. Nayiıhtła did." I pulled away in fear.

"When you got word that your mom died, you stole the car and tried to leave. Maybe to go see her? You were her only child, so the police found you to tell you. To give you the news that you have a bit of an inheritance. Her father's cabin further north."

"No! It can't be!" I struggled as my mind searched wildly to make sense of it all.

"This happens sometimes when we experience too much pain in one lifetime to carry on our own. We need to protect ourselves, protect that scared little child within us, Nayiìhtła." Alice looked me straight in the eyes with compassion and truth.

Nayiìhtła came back to me on our stop at the shale rock beach, on the way back to the reserve.

I thought I heard her laughter in the distance over the sound of the water sweeping the millions of pieces of brittle shale onto the shore with every gentle wave. I looked out the small round window of the boat to see where the noise was coming from and saw her in the middle of the fjord, but she wasn't alone. She was with another girl that looked almost identical to her and an older man in a single-engine boat, going towards the shore. The other girl looked so familiar. I knew her somehow but couldn't place her right away. Her smile. I had only ever seen it once before.

That was when I knew.

Somehow, in some inexplicable way, she was my mother.

And the man, he was the man in my vision.

My grandfather.

They had a dead muskox at the helm. I could see the tip of one of its curved and pointed horns and its thick dark brown coat.

They gassed up at one of the caches hidden in the bushes and went on their way again. Nayiìhtła was the only one who saw me. She waved and smiled. I put my hand up to the window. I felt as though I hadn't seen her in a long time and maybe I hadn't. She was a version of myself I no longer recognized. She was safe now. We were safe. Each of us one and the same in our own time and space across the fire in the place of healing waters.

~

ACKNOWLEDGEMENTS

Mahsi cho to Elder Celine Marlowe from Łutsël K'é for taking the time to read the manuscript. Łutsël K'é and the surrounding Thaidene Nëné National Park was the inspiration for Nyla's healing journey to sacred waters. The original oral story of the Lady of the Falls comes from this area and can be found on the Nation's website. Thank you Steven Nitah for reminding me that the old woman is not only at the Falls but everywhere in Denendeh.

Mahsi cho to Elder Berna Martin for guiding and teaching me about Enodah, the place among the Thousand Islands, the place where you grew up.

Mahsi cho to my grandmother Alice for always showing me the way, even long after you passed on into the spirit world.

Mahsi cho to West Point First Nation for helping me to understand the duties of a Firekeeper.

Mahsi cho to my friends and fellow writers who took the time to review the words within and provide your honest feedback before it was published.

Mahsi cho to Rhonda Kronyk for taking on this work, especially after the tremendous task of helping to get *Land-Water-Sky* to where it needed to be. Your excellent editorial eye is unmatched, and I enjoy working with you.

Mahsi Cho to everyone at Fernwood and Roseway for your hard work in getting this book to print.

Mahsi cho to all the community firefighters up north so bravely putting your lives on the line every day, including my son who inspired me with his stories of what it is like being out on the land fighting an active forest fire.

Mahsi cho to my counsellor, for helping me connect to and nurture my inner child.

Mahsi cho to all the Ancestors who are on the other side of the fire.

~

PREVIOUS PUBLICATIONS

Katłįą has written three previous books with Roseway — two novels and a memoir, *Northern Wildflower,* written as Catherine Lafferty. She has been shortlisted for the Victoria City Book Prize (2023), and her debut novel won the NorthWoods Book Awards (2021).

THIS HOUSE IS NOT A HOME (2022)

> *"Absolutely exquisite. Told with such love and gentle ferocity, I'm convinced this book will never leave those who read it."*
> — RICHARD VAN CAMP, author of *The Lesser Blessed*

An intergenerational coming-of-age novel that follows Kǫ̀, a Dene man who grew up entirely on the land before being taken to residential school. When he finally returns home, he struggles to connect with his family: his younger brother whom he has never met, his mother because he has lost his language, and an absent father whose disappearance he is too afraid to question.

A fictional story based on true events, *This House Is Not a Home* is visceral and embodied, heartbreaking and spirited, presenting a clear trajectory of how settlers dispossessed Indigenous Peoples of their land — and how Indigenous communities, with dignity and resilience, continue to live and honour their culture, values, inherent knowledge systems, and Indigenous rights towards re-establishing sovereignty. Fierce and unflinching, this story is a call for land back.

~ For more on this title, visit *fernwoodpublishing.ca/book/this-house-is-not-a-home*

LAND-WATER-SKY/NDÈ-TI-YAT'A (2020)

> *"This book is so descriptive in the way the Elders told stories that I related to all the events. Mahsı Cho for keeping our stories alive."*
>
> — MARO SUNDBERG, Executive Director at Goyatiko Language Society

A vexatious shapeshifter walks among humans. Shadowy beasts skulk at the edges of the woods. A ghostly apparition haunts a lonely stretch of highway. Spirits and legends rise and join together to protect the North. Set in Canada's far north, this layered composite novel traverses space and time. Riveting, subtle, and unforgettable, Katłà gives us a unique perspective into what the world might look like today if Indigenous legends walked amongst us, disguised as humans, and ensures that the spiritual significance and teachings behind the stories of Indigenous legends are respected and honoured.

~ For more on this title, visit *fernwoodpublishing.ca/book/land-water-sky-nde-t1-yata*

NORTHERN WILDFLOWER (2017)

> *"Lafferty has pulled this off with disarming honesty and grace."*
>
> — QUILL & QUIRE (JANUARY 2018)

Northern Wildflower is a beautifully written and powerful memoir. With startling honesty and a distinct voice, the author tells her story of being a Dene woman growing up in Canada's North and her struggles with intergenerational trauma, discrimination, poverty, addiction, love, and loss. Focusing on the importance of family ties, education, spiritualism, cultural identity, health, happiness, and the courage to speak the truth, Lafferty's words bring cultural awareness and relativity to Indigenous and non-Indigenous readers alike, giving insight into the real issues many Indigenous women face and dispelling misconceptions about what life in the North is like.

~ For more on this title, visit *fernwoodpublishing.ca/book/northern-wildflower*

AN EXCERPT

from *This House Is Not a Home*

≈

CHAPTER 1

K ọ̀ was taught that every animal had a reason for being, but he had great difficulty understanding the purpose of the mosquito. Letting one of the annoying buzzards land on his exposed, balmy skin, he watched the pesky insect curiously. Why was its long stinger designed solely for the purpose of drinking blood? Kọ̀ wondered. Without consent, the insect took as much as it could carry and flew away, low to the ground, heavy with the weight of Kọ̀'s sticky red blood, leaving a cruel itch and a large welt in exchange. Not a fair trade at all, Kọ̀ thought.

It was early morning, still dark, but Kọ̀ and his father were already on the move. Kọ̀ tried to sit still and quietly like his father, but he was restless. Their backs upright and straightened against a towering cold piece of flat slate, they waited for the perfect opportunity to approach the large bull moose they had been following closely for the past day and a half.

≈

Kọ̀ was born in one of the most unforgiving parts of the world. In a place where the cold can kill a man in a matter of minutes. Where one wrong move could end a life. Where there is no room for mistakes, no room for doubt, no room for anything other than survival. Where at the end of the day gratitude sets in. A deep appreciation to Creator. Having lived now for the count of ten winters, Kǫ was thankful to be alive each and every day and grateful for all things Creator made. Kǫ learned from a young age not to let one day go by without giving thanks to Creator. To Kǫ, Creator was the land, and the land was Creator. They were one and the same. For thousands of years, Kǫ's family travelled the vast North. They had many gathering places that spread far and wide in all directions. They knew the best spots to pick berries and where to set traps. They knew where to lower their fishing nets and which migratory routes the caribou would take from year to year. The land was their home. They had many homes. Some areas they travelled to for the summer, other places they would hunker down for the long winter. They had no need to stay in only one place; the entire countryside was theirs to explore. Kǫ's ancestors passed on the knowledge of the land and how to live as one with the land from generation to generation so as not to lose their way of life.

Kǫ developed a sense of pride in knowing how to survive on the land with his heart and his hands, mostly through the teachings of his father. Because of this, Kǫ learned to both love the land and fear it for he knew nothing was as powerful as nature, and for that he respected it greatly. Kǫ studied his father's serious weathered face as they sat together in wait. He couldn't remember the last time his father had spoken other than giving him short orders. His father had no need for words; one look from him told Kǫ all he needed to know. On the land, words had little meaning. Words were weak sounds carried away by the wind, but actions had strength behind them.

The rare time Kǫ's father did speak was when he told stories, stories that Kǫ could not entirely piece together all at once. Kǫ's father was a good storyteller, but Kǫ was often left with many unanswered questions.

"Ts'ehwhį." He was assured by his mother that, in time, he would come to know the ancient teachings in the stories and the meaning behind them, that he would one day be the one to tell those same stories and pass them on to his own children. Everyone Kǫ̀ knew was a storyteller. They all told stories with lessons behind them. Stories were told incrementally, throughout the years, so that the message would become ingrained in the listener, retained for life after an entire lifetime of repetition.

⚹

Kǫ̀'s father started in on one of his stories to pass the time as they sat in the reeds near the mouth of the river at dusk, their two hidden figures blending in perfectly with nature far downstream from the rushing waterfall, in a quiet place where the river lapped into a calm stir. The cascade still towering over them from afar. It was no question to Kǫ̀ that the moose was alive just as much as he was. It lived and breathed. And although beautiful, it was very dangerous. If one were to get too close, one would surely be taken under by the sheer force and power behind it, his father warned. "Hojı." It continuously created its own storm, the rushing current dancing together night and day endlessly.

"Ejìecho eyıts'ǫ hòezıʔejìe deh nąı̀lı łak'a ts'ǫhk'e negı̨̀h?à n̨ıdè, ekò dè asìıdeè goxè ładı agode ha." His father stared out at the waterfall in the distance as he told his son one of the oldest prophesies he knew. It was said that when the two animals, the bison and muskox, from different parts of the land meet on either side of the waterfall it would be a sign of great changes to come.

Get a copy today from your nearest bookstore, or visit us online at *fernwoodpublishing.ca/book/this-house-is-not-a-home.*

Also available as ebook and audiobook.